TILLINGFOLD'S TOUR

Also by John Parker:

THE VILLAGE CRICKET MATCH
TEST TIME AT TILLINGFOLD
CRICKET STYLES AND STYLISTS

TILLINGFOLD'S TOUR

John Parker

W.H. ALLEN · LONDON
1986

Printed and bound in Great Britain by
Mackays of Chatham Ltd, Kent.
for the Publishers, W.H. Allen & Co. Plc
44 Hill Street, London W1X 8LB

British Library Cataloguing in Publication Data

Parker, John, *1926*—
Tillingfold's tour.
I. Title
823′.914 [F] PR6066.A635

ISBN 0–491–03571–3

FOR MARGARET

Chapter One

It was Gauvinier's custom, when he had a problem to face, to turn his back on Tillingfold and climb via the foothills to the steep track that took him up a curving field to the summit of the South Downs. When he had recovered his breath – a procedure that nowadays took him much longer than it had, say, ten years before, he noted wryly – he turned his face to the wind and marched off at light-infantry pace. Even in high summer, the breeze from the Channel was cold enough to blow thought from his mind and the blood from his cheeks and hands. 'Twenty minutes, that's all it takes,' he always told Polly. 'I turn about, lean back on the wind and as the warmth comes back into my fingers my mind begins to work again.'

It was a simple formula, but then Gauvinier had spent many of his fifty years pretending to himself that he was a simple man, not at all the complex and intelligent being he was in reality, inspiring more curiosity than awe in those around him. He knew his passion for cricket, inherited from his father, made him an object of amusement to some and of scorn to others, but even in his more objective moments he was unable to shake off his conviction that there was nothing else to compare with it. Even Polly, who had married him in spite of it, thought him a fanatic. 'You're mad,' she stormed at him. 'Stark, staring mad!'

That was when he'd half-hopped, been half-carried from Albert Jess's Corniche after the Raveley match last season. 'It's nothing, nothing at all. I'll be all right,' he insisted, waving off her anger and her attempt to help him. But it had taken a tumbler of whisky and four aspirins to get him to sleep that night and in the morning he was forced to admit defeat. Polly drove him to the surgery, where a young locum he had never seen before poked and prodded him painfully.

'Six weeks. Six weeks and you'll be right as rain. It's a common sporting injury – a burst blood vessel in the hamstring. You'll go all colours of the rainbow from your hip to your toes but don't worry about it. I'll give you a painkiller. Rest up for a week and then take it easy. How did you do it?'

His pen hovered over his prescription pad as Gauvinier, relieved that he hadn't snapped the hamstring itself, admitted shamefacedly that his foot had slipped on wet grass as he was bending down to stop a cricket ball. Now, stepping out on the turf of the Downs and feeling no effects in his thigh, he recalled his question.

'I'm turning fifty this year, doctor. How long d'you think I should keep it up?'

The doctor grinned. 'Cricket? Who knows? As long as you feel you're able to. The longer the better, in fact. Or as long as they'll let you in the team.'

He checked his walk and looked south to the glint of the April sun off the sea. The memory lived with him of that month's enforced absence from the team, when he'd handed over to Fred Bason and he'd told Polly that he thought people had begun to mutter behind his back.

'I'm sure you're imagining it, Peter,' she said. 'In any case, Tillingfold's always talked behind people's backs. You've lived here all your life and you should be used to it by now.'

'But I *am* fifty. Perhaps I should pack it in and let someone else have a go.'

'Peter. You know no one else would do the job you do for the club and for the village. Who could take over?'

'Oh, Fred could. Or Albert. No one's indispensable, you know.' But he sounded so forlorn that Polly laughed at him and packed him off to the Dog and Duck for a pint of bitter with his friend, Oliver Fanshawe, chairman of the Tillingfold Cricket Club and its groundsman and umpire. Fanshawe was preoccupied.

'You've got plenty of time before you need to make any decision. Don't be so damned silly, Peter. You're as active as two other men in the field half your age. Rhodes played for England when he was fifty, you know.' Fanshawe was an amateur cricket historian of some distinction. 'What you should be exercising your mind on is this damned tour. And that damned girl of yours.'

So these were two more problems that Gauvinier had brought to stride out with him in the wind blowing off the Channel on a cold February morning. James Mitterman, the club's treasurer, who had connections in the City, had made the suggestion at the annual general meeting in October that Tillingfold should emulate other, bigger clubs and make a three or four match tour in some other part of the country.

Mitterman suggested Devonshire, and it transpired that a couple of business acquaintances had made such a tour. Over gin-and-tonics at the Inn on the Park they had persuaded Mitterman that the West Country was a Mecca of fast wickets and good beer; besides, they added, there was a proposed new development just outside Exeter in which it might be of benefit for Mitterman to invest. Mitterman, whose expeditions outside London and the south-east of England were usually limited to Switzerland in the skiing season and the lesser Greek islands in the summer, and who liked to combine pleasure with his business, was convinced. In fact, without consulting the other members of the committee, he had gone so far towards committing Tillingfold actually to making the tour that the club could not withdraw without considerable embarrassment.

You had to hand it to James, thought Gauvinier. He had the hide of a rhinoceros. The man had stood up in his dark grey pinstripe, leaning with the tops of his fingers gently on the top of his briefcase, shirtcuffs not quite hiding a gold Omega wristwatch, indifferent to the puzzlement on the faces watching him.

'. . . and so you see, I have all the details here,' he ended smoothly, 'I've had them replicated for you to study. You'll find a list of the clubs and the dates on which we'll be playing them, the names of motels and boarding houses and their telephone numbers if you want to make your own arrangements, and an estimated costing for the trip, rather depending on how many of us want to go. All I require is a sufficient number of names of those interested and a cheque for £25 a head as a deposit and I'll go ahead and make the arrangements. It should run out in the end at about £50 each for accommodation and food, plus what you spend in the bar. We need at least fourteen players, plus an umpire and scorer if possible.'

There was a moment of absolute silence in the pavilion, followed by a collective intake of breath. Fanshawe, in the chair, stilled the impending confusion of tongues with an upraised hand.

'I'm sure we'll all thank Mr Mitterman for troubling himself so much on our behalf. What he's said is very interesting but I must say it breaks new ground for Tillingfold. We've always been a village team with no aspirations to anything more – er – elevated. There are many questions to be gone into if we are to contemplate anything so ambitious as Mr Mitterman suggests. I'm sure he will agree' – a quick inquiring glance in the secretary's direction – 'that the best course would be for the committee to consider the matter and come forward with a full proposal. But perhaps the meeting would like to express some views on the subject.'

Gauvinier remained silent. As captain of the club he had long since learned the value of holding his tongue and assessing the balance of opinion before taking action. On the field he was a shrewd, positive and occasionally inspiring captain; off it, he preferred, like the Duke of Plaza Toro, to lead his regiments from behind. He found it less exacting. As often happens, the meeting found itself swept along on the tide of enthusiasm generated by the younger members of the side, led by Paul White and Edward Trine. Only Bason voiced the reservations of the old guard of Tillingfold faithfuls, rounding on Mitterman in his blunt way for breaking the time-honoured tradition of government by committee by 'actin' without authority, that's what you'm done, James. Actin' without authority. What about the youngsters? They ha'nt got money like that.

They'll never afford it. We won't get a side up. Doan't know I can afford time, any road. How are we goin' to get a team together at all, come to that? There's enough trouble now puttin' out two teams of a Sunday.'

Gauvinier knew Bason would never pass up the chance of such a trip and in any case was his own master and a building contractor who could afford to buy up most of the team (except maybe Jess and Trine and Mitterman and certainly Fanshawe, who could not be bought by anyone). However, he shared some of Bason's misgivings, particularly because he would have to take the bulk of the responsibility; but the other Gauvinier, the part of him that rose to any challenge, brushed them aside and he heard himself saying: 'Well, you know, it's not a bad idea after all. And James has done so much groundwork that all we've got to do is to make a go of it.' He paused. 'But there's one thing. We've still got over £1,000 in the bank, and I'm sure the trustees would be persuaded to let us use some of that to cut down the individual costs. I propose the committee looks into it and reports back to a special general meeting in a month's time.'

Amid a chorus of 'hear, hears' the meeting had adjourned to the Dog and Duck, as Tillingfold meetings usually did, and now Gauvinier was walking the Downs mulling over the tour and its problems. Thank the Lord, he said to himself, that Mitterman would handle the finances. Gauvinier had once run a raffle and had found himself paying in £10 of his own money to square the books.

Stories of the exploits of cricket teams on tour circulate through the game gathering momentum as they travel. Although he had never been on a tour himself, Gauvinier was well versed in the tales of broken-down transport, washed-out matches, drinking sprees and near-fatal injuries. He had never quite believed the story of the team that set out from South London for Long Sutton in Lincolnshire only to find their coach pulling up, precisely on time, at the cricket ground in Long Sutton, Somerset. But he had been assured earnestly on three separate occasions that it was true. Tillingfold itself had entertained the occasional touring club in the past, although the fixture list was so full these days that the club had rather shied away from extra matches. The best-laid of squares cannot take too many games in a season, and Fanshawe lavished a mother's care on his pitches. But apart from one young gentleman who had been offensively sick in the roadway outside the Dog and Duck Gauvinier had found the cricketing marauders to be quite unexceptional folk, and if there had been any complaints of molestation from the Tillingfold lasses, Gauvinier was unaware of them.

The selection committee – Bason, Fanshawe and himself – had still to decide upon the composition of the touring party. Thirteen of Tillingfold's paid-up playing members had volunteered for the trip, which surprised the committee as it was felt that many of the younger unemployed fellows could not afford the £25; so far only Paul White had applied confidentially for the committee's financial aid, and the whole of Tillingfold knew that his meter-reader's take home pay of £75 a week was hardly enough to cover his expenditure on whisky and cigarettes, let alone the hire-purchase instalments on his 1,000 cc Honda and the girls from Billington with multi-coloured hair and expensive tastes in bad clothes and worse cocktails. But as the village said more often than not, when discussing the

Whites, Paul's late father had done very nicely, thank you. The old man, whose father had been a head gardener and his father before him, had spent his working life in the grounds of Tillingfold Manor, working for the Trine family, and his spare time with his own rosebeds. Although he had never tried to grow roses for a profit, their propagation and breeding had fascinated him since he was a lad. After years of experimentation, cross-pollination, cross-grafting, culling, rejecting and selecting, old Cliff had produced White's Black at the age of seventy-one, when Paul was fifteen. Three years later White's Black won a Special Award at the Chelsea Flower Show and for the first time in his life Cliff White had fame and a little fortune to spare. With the contrariness that had marked his batting all his life, he promptly died, leaving a comfortable annuity for his wife, and £50 and a copy of the Ten Commandments for Paul. That young man, rather to his own surprise, bought a cricket bat with the cash (Gray-Nicolls, £45, a beauty), thrust the Commandments under his socks in a drawer in his bedroom, and set out cheerfully to break as many of them as possible in the shortest possible time – with the exception of the Seventh; young Paul considered you had to be married to commit adultery, and at twenty-one he had many years of freedom to come. As for the Tillingford ladies and those of the surrounding villages, he didn't mind if *they* were committing adultery or not. He looked forward to the tour as a new adventure packed with possibilities.

Gauvinier ticked them off in his mind. Himself, Mitterman of course, the irrepressible Jess, Fred Bason, Frank Hunter – 'Fred'n'Frank' as they were known to the village – Bill Budgeon (good old reliable

Bill, wish we had more like him), Edward Trine the Squire's son and his cousin Rupert, Paul White and Tillingfold's other really promising young cricketer, the fast bowler Norman Smith, who'd had a trial for the county. The there was young Bobby Bewers, who'd scored for Tillingfold since he was ten and was now fourteen and as good a batsman as any they'd got in the side, as well as a promising leg-spinner, Joe Deacon, the little Cockney milkman-wicketkeeper with his hands as fast as his tongue and a penchant for King and Barnes bitter, the carpenter Colin Verrall (who'd presented Tillingfold with the wooden platters that had added so much character to the club's famous teas) and the Reverend Richard Veysey, Vicar of Tillingfold. And there was Gillian Grantham, 'that damned girl of yours,' as Fanshawe had described her.

Miss Grantham had turned up at Tillingfold's nets a couple of seasons before and, having floored Albert Jess with an inswinging ball to the box, had demanded to be admitted as a playing member of the Tillingfold CC. Indeed, she had proferred immediate payment of the subscription, which was unusual in itself. There was something about the set of her jaw and the levelness of her eye that led Gauvinier to believe that, had she been refused, she might well have taken the case to the Equal Opportunities Board, the Human Rights Commission and, if necessary, the European Court at The Hague. Fortunately there had been no such necessity. The players, recognising a sportsman when they saw one (Miss Grantham was wearing jeans at the time) took her off to the Dog and Duck, and only some of the older vice-presidents had demurred at the special meeting Gauvinier had called to discuss the matter. Oliver Fanshawe, whose own brand of logic made sense of both Enoch Powell and Tony Benn at one and the same time, was by far the strongest opponent of Miss Grantham's admission to the club. The matter had soured his relationship with Gauvinier for the first time since they had both vied for the affections of a certain Tillingford belle before the war.

'A cricket field's no place for a girl, except to decorate the boundary or make the teas.' (Didactically.)

'Oh, come off it, Oliver.' (Scornfully.) 'That sort of reasoning went out with the ark.'

'I mean it, Peter.' (Earnestly.) 'It's a man's game. Letting women in will only debase it. They haven't the same strength as men. And besides, what about the ball?'

'What about it?' Knowing full well what Fanshawe meant.

'It's too hard. Women are afraid of it.'

'Not this one, Oliver. You've picked the wrong lass.'

'But where are you going to put her in the field? Even if a woman can bat and bowl a bit,' he added grudgingly, 'they certainly can't throw in from the boundary.'

'Nor can half the side,' Gauvinier said grimly. 'I have the devil of a job trying to hide James – and some of the other blighters.' He recalled vividly the day a couple of seasons ago when he had led the reluctant Mitterman by the hand to the exact spot where he wished him to field and marked the spot with a penny. Gauvinier could stomach a bad fielder, but not one who didn't try. 'In any case, she's as sharp as anyone in the team and she can take a slip catch, too.'

'Yes, I suppose she can,' said Fanshawe, who was to see the young lady in question swoop like a swallow to pick up a low fast catch off the bowling of

Norman Smith, who was as fast as anyone he knew in the county. 'But what's to happen in the dressing room, Peter? You can't have mixed changing.'

'Why ever not? If the girl doesn't mind I'm sure the chaps won't.'

'It's . . . It's . . . not decent.'

'For God's sake, Oliver, what age are you living in? This is the twentieth century. The birds and the bees went out with Victoria. I'd never have thought to hear you, of all people . . . perhaps it's just as well you never married.'

He regretted it the moment he said it. Fanshawe had been engaged when he was shot down and badly injured during the Battle of Britain. He was told he would live with a permanent limp and constant pain, and could never have children. In spite of his fiancée's pleading (she had a blonde bob and violet eyes), he had forced her to break the engagement and look elsewhere. They had been very much in love. For thirty years Fanshawe had lived alone, with Wisden as his comfort.

Fanshawe rose in his customary stiff manner, but his eyes were colder than Gauvinier had ever seen them. He felt like a worm on the end of a pin. But all Fanshawe said was: 'I'm sorry you said that, Peter,' and walked from the pub.

'Shit,' muttered Gauvinier under his breath, for he rarely swore. He then ordered a double scotch. That night Polly bullied him and made him promise to make it up with his friend. But she teased him too. She had met Miss Grantham. 'That girl's going to fall for you, Peter, if you're not careful,' she said.

'Don't be daft,' Gauvinier snapped, his touchiness heightened by the knowledge that in the past he had proved not unattractive to the female sex, and that he was by no means immune to temptation even though fast approaching his own half-century. Polly smiled. 'I know you,' she said a shade maliciously. 'Just you wait and see.'

But so far, Miss Grantham had posed unexpectedly little threat to the smooth running of Tillingfold CC, beyond some mutterings in the village. Tillingfold's traditional opponents, the villages about that part of Sussex, were wont to make suggestive remarks at first, but the news of her twenty-nine and two catches against Raveley, and her three wickets for eighteen against Billington Second Eleven had soon spread to all quarters of the county via the *County Times* weekly reports. White's importunate approaches had been coolly and skilfully rebuffed, much to that young man's chagrin, and no one else in the team had 'tried anything on', in the old Sussex phrase. The players had soon become accustomed to the curly-haired girl in the short white skirt with the sturdy tanned legs running up to bowl slow-medium 'floaters' which had a habit of skidding faster off the pitch than expected. Far from being a liability, she soon became something of a mascot. She had even softened Fanshawe's stony opinions by expertly unscrewing the carburettor from Tillingfold's ancient motor mower, then blowing through the jets before cleaning out the float chamber with an old rag wrapped round a screwdriver and reassembling the motor. 'There,' she told Fanshawe, raising her voice over the rattle of the two-stroke, 'try it now.' And he had to admit that the thirty-year-old machine had never run so sweetly.

And so far, Gauvinier thought, the sex thing had not raised its ugly head. But what might come to pass on the intimacy of a tour, he wondered? And in whose cars would they travel? Or would it be better to take a coach? What about paying for the petrol? One or two players were notorious for 'forgetting' their dues. Who would score? It would be term time and the Bewers kids would be at school. That was a point – so would young Bobby. How could he have applied? Billington Grammar would hardly give him a week off school, and Gauvinier was not going to countenance, let alone connive at, truancy – was he? Who would take the kit? Would his middle-aged Vauxhall stand the journey? Would Polly come too? They'd need a new bag. And some stumps, two or three new sets of pads, and so on. Which of the firms would give them the best deal? Jess was pretty good at that sort of bargaining. What sort of a girl was Gillian Grantham? He didn't know much about her, except that she'd been at one of the more solid girls' schools and had been at Loughborough, which accounted for her all-round sporting ability. He didn't even know what she did for a living, only that she had arrived a year or so back with her widowed mother to live in a cottage in one of the more remote hamlets along the Downs. Aveley, or Albury, he wasn't sure. Should they take her on tour or not?

A swift shadow crossed the overbright sun and a gust of wind whipped at Gauvinier's back as a squall of wet sleet hit the back of his head and legs. Thankfully, he turned back down under the lee of the hill and ran and slithered most of the mile down to the village whose lights in the sudden gloom looked so inviting. It was a quarter to one. Just time for a pint of King and Barnes Festive ale, admirable on a day like this, before Polly's rabbit stew. It was only as he sank the last drop of the heavy, heady brew that he realised that he hadn't answered any of the questions he had taken to the top of the Downs. And the Tour Committee meeting was due to be held tonight, in the skittle bar at the back of this very same public house.

And he would be fifty in two weeks' time.

Chapter Two

It seemed to Gauvinier that he was taking a very long time to make up his mind exactly where to stand at first slip. It mattered to him, for he took his cricket more seriously perhaps than any other part of his life, that he should not be found too far back from the batsman when the ball took one of those wickedly low edges; or too close so that a sudden flier might cause him to snatch at the catch and miss, possibly at the cost of a badly bruised finger. At the bowler's end Norman Smith was still pacing out his run. Gauvinier moved a couple of paces forward, studying the strange pitch. It was odd, he felt, now this day had come that he had been looking forward to with anticipation mounting almost to excitement, that there should be this feeling of indecision, almost of staleness. Perhaps it was merely the fact that here he was, leading Tillingfold into a cricket match as he had done half a thousand times before, but for the first time not in the cosy familiar Sussex Weald, but deep in the heart of Gloucestershire. He knew nothing of the village of Wym, nor of its team, except that Mitterman had told him, when accepting the fixture: 'They're a sort of grace and favour team – they play on the Lord of the Manor's ground and they're a mixed bunch. They've got a couple of big hitters, apparently, and are quite likely to sport a couple of Blues. The pitch isn't supposed to be up to much but the beer's good and strong.' Gauvinier wished he hadn't taken the second pint of the local brew after the coach disgorged, shook his head and looked again at the pitch. Not much good was a euphemism he thought, studying the coarse brown turf with, just short of a length at one end, a large rich green patch of moss.

'Oi'm sorry about the wicket,' Brown, the Wym skipper told him in a rich Gloucestershire accent, shaking him warmly by the hand as he stepped off the coach. 'There's been the worst drought this century down here, and they won't let us water. Old Cowper – that's our groundsman – he's in a real taking.' he laughed a rich West Country laugh and marched Gauvinier and his team into the Shepherd's Crook. 'Now I've put a jug or two up for the lads so's you won't worry too much about the pitch later on.' And when two hours later he flipped a coin neatly into the middle of the mossy patch and Gauvinier could have sworn he caught the flash of a double-head, Brown laughed his big laugh again and told Gauvinier: 'We'll field' – a pause – 'after tea, when its cooler.' Hospitality, Gauvinier wondered, seasoned with the cricketer's will to win, perhaps. He eyed the patch of moss and moved back two deliberate paces, motioning to Deacon, the keeper, and Hunter at second slip, to stand back a bit with him.

He flexed his knees a couple of times, loosening the leg muscles, and glanced round at the disposition of his fielders. His cricketer's mind passed over without registering the magnificent setting of Wym CC's ground, perched high on a piece of rolling Cotswold, with chestnut oaks standing like outposts of the big house, casting their centuries-old shade in green pools, in which basked the Earl of Wym's pedigree Guernseys, flicking their tails at the flies. The drought-browned grass stretched away in folds as the hills climbed towards Wym House, which stood Parthenon-like with its pillars against the blue horizon half a mile away. Round the cricket field itself a stout chestnut fence had been lined with wire netting to keep out the marauding flocks of sheep which roamed ceaselessly, seemingly oblivious to the hot sun under their shaggy coats. There was a scattering of applause from the direction of the pavilion, and Gauvinier collected his thoughts before calling loudly 'Man in' and leading the *obligator* as the two home batsmen strode jauntily towards the wicket.

Forty yards away, Norman Smith paced out his run for the third time. '. . . thirteen . . . fourteen . . . fifteen . . .' He turned on his right heel and dug into his pocket for the little flat plate with its spike that he carried with him to every match. The home team, of course, was supposed by custom and practice to supply the bowler's markers, but Norman had found that at this level it didn't always apply. As a countryman himself he had an aversion to tearing a mark in the turf with his spikes (which in any case got clogged by such a habit) and the first time he had taken his own marker to a match he had taken his first hat-trick. So his marker had become one of those little superstitions which grow on cricketers like warts. He wheeled his right arm thoughtfully, in much the same reflex as Gauvinier had done his knee-bends.

This was an important match for Norman, in more ways than one. It was the first time he'd left Bella and their baby son, and he hadn't really wanted to go on Tillingfold's tour. But Bella had persuaded him, her logic matching the love in her heart for this, her big baby. Five years ago Norman had been spoken of around the Sussex villages in similar tones of awe to those accorded thirty years before to his father Stan and thirty years before that to his Uncle Syd. 'Best bowler in the county,' they said and, surpassing his forebears, Norman had been offered and had accepted a year's trial at Hove. But there he had been told that his action was too 'chest-on' and the coaches had spent hours getting his run-up right, ensuring his right arm brushed against his right ear as his left shoulder pointed towards the batsman. After three matches with the county second XI, during which time he took four wickets and one catch, Norman was only too glad to return to Tillingfold and his job at the stables. Gauvinier – furious but not particularly surprised – had welcomed him back with open arms. Young Smith was so disillusioned with 'the big time' that he turned down approaches from major clubs like Raveley and Billington – and, yes, even Horsham – to open the bowling for their League sides, and indeed, Gauvinier had thought, it was just as well. The young man's confidence had vanished. His easy run to the wicket, smooth swing over of the arm and natural swerve of the ball had been subordinated to a knees-up, elbows in, waggling imitation of the former England Captain, Bob Willis. Admittedly, he bowled faster than he had before, but the subtlety and control which had marked him as a coming man seemed no longer a part of his make-up as a bowler.

'God knows what they think they're doing down at Hove,' Gauvinier grumbled to Fanshawe. 'They take a boy with all the natural talent in the world and coach it all out of him on some bloody silly theory that all people are alike. And yet they're the county which has had great individualists like Maurice Tate.'

'And look what they did to him in the end.' Fanshawe was not a cricket historian for nothing. 'But I agree with you, Peter. What are you going to do with Norman?

'Teach him to bat,' said Gauvinier. And indeed he did. Over the next three seasons he paid particular attention to the straightness of the young man's bat in the nets, the positioning of his feet on the drive, and so on. He left his bowling strictly alone. And over the three years Norman Smith slowly recovered his rhythm and his confidence, until now once more he could be relied on to open Tillingfold's bowling and carry on clean through an innings if desired; the subtle late swing of the ball had come back, and so had the unexpected nip off the pitch, and Norman Smith was once more spoken of through the Sussex villages as 'the best in the county'. But so far he'd never taken wickets in the wide world outside, and Wym (though he'd never heard of it before) was where he was determined to begin. Norman mentally tipped his hat, with a little twinge in his heart, to Bella and the baby back in the Tillingfold cottage, and then forgot all about them as he glanced around the field and waved James Mitterman back a yard or two at square leg.

Obediently, Mitterman retired to the required position, albeit with his natural expression of disapproval pulling down the corners of his mouth. Norman, like most of the younger members of the team (except Paul White, of course) could not bring himself to say 'James'. It was always 'Mr Mitterman', and there was no doubt that the secretary-treasurer had brought dignity and style to the Tillingfold team. Mitterman allowed his quite enormous self-confidence to override the fact that he was a poor cricketer with less natural ability than anyone else in the side. He smoothed down the long sleeve of his cream silk shirt and brushed an imaginary speck of dirt from the razor crease of his flannels (bought for the tour from Simpson's in Piccadilly). A good thing someone showed the flag for Tillingfold, he thought to himself, watching the batsman take guard. He ran over in his mind the arrangements he'd made for the tour: the fixtures; the transport; the collecting of the money (God, you'd think these people didn't have a penny to bless themselves with); the accommodation; every little detail down to the counting of the pads and bats in the club bag. You'd think the skipper could have done *that*, at least, thought Mitterman, who regarded Gauvinier as a romantic, which indeed he was. 'I don't know what the Club would do without me,' he added to himself with some resentment, for a willing horse is often likely to regard itself as hard done by.

But he was right, for although he had joined the village cricket club when he had come to Tillingfold in order to ingratiate himself with the local VIPs, like the Trines and Albert Jess, his financier's mind and accountant's training had enabled him to rescue the club from near bankruptcy and place it in the enviable position where it could now venture into new realms – like this tour. In his heart, James Mitterman could admit that he owed his place in the team to his ability to juggle figures rather than his ball-sense, but in his own way he had come to love Tillingfold – and cricket – just as much as Gauvinier, or Fanshawe, or young White slouching there in the covers. Not that James Mitterman would ever have said so out loud, or have admitted that in fact a fast-moving cricket ball frightened him so much that he was always pleased to be moved a few yards further from the batsman. There were a number of people in Tillingfold, as there were in the City, who would have given a great deal to know that James Mitterman, financier, wheeler-dealer and asset-stripper, envied and – yes – respected anyone who could face four and a half ounces of moving red leather without flinching. Even young White, fidgeting restlessly out there at cover point, or crippled Bill Budgeon in the scorebox. Or Gill – Gillian Grantham, librarian at Billingham, half a dozen miles from Tillingfold, graduate of Loughborough in Physical Education and English, and Tillingfold's second change bowler and gully fielder.

It had taken Gill, aided and abetted by Gauvinier, some three months to be admitted to Tillingfold Cricket Club; as a playing member a slightly shorter time to convince Gauvinier that she was worth her place in the team; and two matches and a bowling average of three for seventeen in ten overs against Warninglid to persuade the rest of the team to accept her on level terms. Perhaps it helped that Miss Grantham (she firmly eschewed the modern Ms) did not have the figure to grace Page Three of the *Sun*, and spent rather less at the hairdresser than she did at the sports shop. Perhaps it was because her wide grey eyes somehow embarrassed the gauche presumptive approaches of Paul White, as well as the more subtle advances of the older men, without anything being said. More probably, Gauvinier thought, it was because in some form of minor miracle, Gillian Grantham was completely besotted, as he and Fanshawe and Jess and Bason, and even Mitterman and White and the rest were, with cricket.

It had taken Tillingfold's opponents longer than Tillingfold's own players to accept a girl of twenty-two as a 'proper' cricketer. Being bowled out by a girl, it seemed, was the worst indignity a cricketer could be called to undergo. And somehow it seemed to be all her fault. As indeed it was. But around the villages of the Sussex Weald Gillian Grantham had quite soon ceased to be a name to cause astonishment; indeed, she was greeted with an amused tolerance by most of the men, which in its way was more insulting than outright opposition. 'It's like being a token black,' she stormed at Gauvinier, and all he could reply was: 'Stick it out. They'll get used to you,' in not too convincing a tone, thankful at least that the worst of his worries appeared not to have been realised.

The reaction of Brown, the Wym skipper, to the news that his visitors from farthest Sussex numbered a girl in their side had been typical. 'Well, I don't know about that,' he said, his gentle Gloucestershire accent revealing his puzzlement. 'I've never heard of such a thing . . . well, mornin' to you, miss.' His large brown hand had enveloped Gillian's. 'You sure you'll be all right?' And he had had no answer to her rather sharp: 'Why not?' but turned away with a baffled expression.

Fielding at gully, Gillian Grantham smoothed down her short white skirt with an unconsciously feminine action, ignoring and yet conscious of Paul White's eyes on her athlete's brown legs. Out at cover point, White fidgeted back and forth with the loose-limbed movements of the born fielder. He too was conscious of Gillian, even though, he thought, I'm getting used to her now. At heart, Paul White was a much more shy young man than his public image would suggest. In his thoughts, much of the language which so annoyed Gauvinier and other elders was transmuted to 'pp' in place of the usual 'ff'; and although he would rather have died than admit it, he was somewhat in awe of the girl. She wasn't like the exotic birds with their garish hairstyles who giggled in the pubs, nor yet the eager furtive housewives who invited him to 'Come in and have a cup of tea' when he was on his meter rounds. It was all wrong, of course, a girl playing cricket, but then Paul was not intelligent enough to realise that even though he might sport the tightest jeans and the shiniest leather shoes, there is none quite so conservative as the young male, no matter how he might rail against Tory misrule. Which is why Paul White, leader of the Tillingfold louts, in his heart of hearts thought it was wrong for a girl to be playing cricket; and his dislike of the situation, not so much of the girl herself, emerged in louche behaviour and suggestive remarks. But he couldn't go too far, or he knew Gauvinier would drop him from the team, for all his ability. And he had to admit that she'd done a helluva sight better than he'd expected. Why, the girl could even throw, not with his own long flat *swiiiish* of a throw from the boundary, to be sure, but from anywhere up to thirty or forty yards it was smack into the wicketkeeper's gloves; and she only needed one bounce from the boundary. He watched her surreptitiously, stretching and bending like any man limbering up before the game.

Frank Hunter watched her too from second slip and thought lewd thoughts to which he considered he was entitled by virtue of his forty-five years and burgeoning paunch. 'God, what I couldn't do if I was ten years younger,' he said to himself, safe in the knowledge that Rose was two hundred miles away and that he was hardly the man for Miss Grantham. Ten years ago he'd taken eight wickets for twenty-five runs against Raveley, Tillingfold's best-ever bowling average, according to Fanshawe, who kept immaculate records. But that was before the garage had first prospered and then been struck by disaster – 'Hope that young bugger remembers to check the pumps and lock'em tonight' – and Fred, his best friend, had been forced to bail him out. For Rose's sake, mind, not for Frank's. For Frank had stolen and married his best friend's childhood sweetheart and things had never been the same between them since. The rivalry between Frank'n'Fred, or Fred'n'Frank, depending on which side you took, continued to feed the Tillingfold gossips after twenty years. But Frank, the early winner in the race for the girl, might well be said to be losing the longer and more difficult game of life. Fred Bason, they said in Tillingfold, was worth ten Franks. And, some of them added, not only in money.

So Frank Hunter lusted and fretted and wondered if he'd brought enough cash with him to see the tour through, while Fred Bason settled his ample backside at short mid-on and studied the earnest young Wym opening batsman expertly marking his guard with the toe of his boot. From his position twelve yards from the bat, Bason could see every detail of the browned grass of the pitch, rolled deceptively flat and matted with the dark green moss showing through. 'Must have a word with Guv,' he thought, but then he saw Gauvinier shuffling back slightly and motioning Hunter on his right and Joe Deacon, the wicket-keeper, to withdraw a little from the wicket. 'Peter doesn't miss much,' thought Bason. 'Ball could be flying about a bit, 'specially if young Norman's on target.'

Fred Bason was wont to take a pessimistic view of matters, which might explain why his construction and development business was rated as one of the soundest little concerns in the south, while the TILLINGFOLD MOTORS sign (Prop: F. Hunter) was missing its initial letter and Frank was still forecasting optimistically: 'It'll be OK when we get our digital pumps.' And the bank manager in Billingham, a bright young man up from Shoreham, had tapped his blotter with a pencil and commented: 'That's all very well, Mr Hunter, but we can't . . .'

Joe Deacon shook his head behind the wicket and wished, not for the first time, that he'd not had those two extra pints in the pub. Strong brew, this West Country beer. Better than the stuff they served up at the Dog and Duck at home. That little Italian girl in Lancing Street, now. She'll be game for a bit when her hubby is away. Her eyes had given him the old one-two when he dropped the milk round yesterday. Thank God he was away from Maisie and the kids for a weekend. Not the life for a man: up in the morning at 4.30 for the milk round; plastering walls for Bason in the afternoon (cash down, of course, no tax); daughters pestering you in the evening; Maisie wanting money and yet more money, it seemed. Not like Jess, him and his fancy woman, little Joe thought with unaccustomed bitterness. He was not usually jealous of the lilac Rolls Royce or the timbered country seat, symbols of a meteoric career in the pop world. But the Spanish soprano, the blonde American tennis player and the Brazilian heiress had each in turn dazzled Tillingfold with their beauty; and Joe Deacon, Lothario manqué, found it quite easy to wonder what it was, if anything, that gave Albert Jess the right to do publicly what he, Deacon, could only do in furtive secret meetings behind hastily opened doors and with sly condemning eyes watching behind half-drawn curtains.

Jess could have told him, but the former teenage idol had nothing on his prematurely lined mind than the sheer pleasure of anticipating a good game. That he was on an English field, brown rather than green, was enough for Jess. He'd learned in forty-five-odd years – very odd, some of them, when he recalled the weeks in the Combi, cheek by jowl with the group and the gear, and the Hollywood Bowl, and Wembley and Woodstock with the braying thousands – to take the days one by one. And cricket and good music, he had discovered to his never-ending delight and surprise, were the two things that made life really worth living. Perhaps, out here in the deep, he'd get one of those steepling catches, or one of those zingers off the full face of the bat . . .' or perhaps it would go to that lucky young bugger Trine, down there on the boundary at fine leg, and already, Jess could see with some amusement, quite preoccupied with the charms of a long-legged girl in jodhpurs, shining black riding boots and an expensive cream silk shirt.

Trine, who had never been known to be diffident, took one look at the square shoulders, silver-blonde hair and high cheekbones, and thought, 'Oh-oh, the aristocracy deigning to visit the peasants.' On the pretext he was seeking the exact position in the field, he edged over towards where she was leaning elegantly on the wooden fence.

'Hullo,' he said, with that particular inflection on the second syllable which implies surprise, recognition and pleasure all at once. 'What are *you* doing here?' He had never seen her before in his life.

She held his eye for long enough to take the sting out of her reply. The Trines of this world are irresistible, after all.

'Watching what promises to be a rather boring game,' she said.

'Are you from up there?' Trine asked, abandoning pretence and nodding across the broad acres to Wym House on the horizon. 'Are you one of the Wyms?'

'Mmm,' she answered, acknowledging his directness. 'I'm Quincey. Quincey Wym. They all call me Quim.' She paused. 'Hadn't you better get on with the game?'

Trine was still digesting this conversation twenty minutes later when he dropped what was for him, a sitter. But when he looked round again, she had gone.

The Reverend Richard Veysey, presiding over the

cricketing section of his flock with massive although uncertain authority at mid-off, was thinking of socks, not sex. His own socks, in fact. When he had stretched his legs out into the coach's gangway on their way down the motorway that morning, he had noticed that he had on one blue and one grey sock. Furthermore, when he unpacked his suitcase (he'd given his cricket bag to Bobby Bewers five years ago in a fit of generosity since regretted) he had found in addition to three pairs of pants, three white cricketing shirts, a spare pair of white flannels, a pair of greys, two spare dog-collars and his Oriel neckerchief, three vests, his razor, toothbrush, a bar of soap and a large brown towel ('White'll get so dirty, dear, and you know what you are'); there were no spare socks. Not even white ones. So perforce he would have to buy some socks on the morrow, on their way to the second match, for today under his flannels and, he hoped desperately, not to be displayed to public view, his ankles were covered by one blue and one grey sock. Especially, he thought, Gillian musn't see them. Though why the good opinions of a girl of twenty-two whom he hardly knew should matter he, fortunately, had not stopped to ask. He tucked in his shirt severely, hoping the little triangle of flesh where he bulged at the navel didn't show, either. He wondered if Oliver Fanshawe ever forgot his socks, or had such disturbing thoughts. Fanshawe would have made a much better vicar than he . . .

The man in question, Fanshawe, looked at his watch and shifted his weight slightly on his shooting stick. He wondered if his pain would lessen if they replaced his aluminium hip with a plastic one, as they'd promised. He wondered if he could afford the operation – they couldn't do it on the National Health, he'd been told, even for Squadron-Leader Oliver Fanshawe, DSO and Bar, DFC and Bar. But then his pain and his near poverty were the two things that never went away; and as so often Oliver Fanshawe shut both his mind and body to them and allowed his whole being to be absorbed into the only thing that made it worth living after all.

'Play!' said Fanshawe.

Chapter Three

NORMAN SMITH'S RUN-UP to the wicket began, as with many other fast bowlers, with a quite unconscious mannerism. Without realising that he did it, he took a widish pace to his left, lifted on his toes, and set off for the bowling crease with three stuttering short steps, rather like Mickey Mouse gathering speed from a static position. Over the next twelve paces to the wicket, his right hand dipped beside him, holding the ball, middle finger firmly along the seam. It was a smooth run-up, gathering pace, his eyes firmly fixed on the mystic patch about four feet in front of the batsman which all cricketers know as 'a good length.' The last pace lenghtened out into a long stride, the left arm straight up in the air with the hand flat and taut like a shark's fin, for balance; the body twisted so the left shoulder pointed directly down the wicket towards the batsman. The boot thumped down squarely across the popping crease, and as the body twisted back evenly the right arm swept over, brushing the right ear, delivering the ball with the whip of the wrist that was Norman's own secret weapon. He knew it was this that gave him that little extra speed off the pitch, the occasional late, late swing of the ball or movement off the seam which had deceived so many batsmen in the past.

Like any good bowler, Norman Smith accomplished his complicated feat of coordination of mind and muscle with a fluidity of movement that made it seem like the easiest thing in the world. And the ball was a beauty. Shining in the sunlight, it flashed like a small red bomb, pitching square in the centre of the patch of moss some five feet in front of the batsman, and dead on the leg stump. The batsman, already and quite correctly on his back foot in front of the wicket, stabbed hastily at it, startled by its sudden pace off the wicket, its lift and slight swing in towards him. Instinctively his body flinched, anticipating a blow in the box, and the ball whisked through twixt bat and body with an audible 'snick', straight to Deacon.

The keeper, taking the ball without thought cleanly in front of his chest, paused a split second in delight and leapt to his full height, a huge grin on his monkey-face and a Tarzan-like roar issuing from his mouth: 'HAAAT!' The confident demand rattled through the pavilion and lost itself in the beech trees. Only one person on the field, including the Wym opening batsman himself, did not believe that he would instantly be walking back to the pavilion.

'Not out,' said umpire Fanshawe, firmly. He removed one shiny pebble from his left pocket and placed it gently in the right one, seeing but not noticing the look on Deacon's face as he tossed the ball dejectedly to Gauvinier; instant gloom replacing instant joy. 'I'm bloody sure he touched that one,' the wicketkeeper muttered – to himself, not out loud, for Gauvinier would not tolerate bad language on the pitch.

Deacon still recalled the look Gauvinier had given

him years ago. For more than three hours he'd stood behind the stumps while Troughton, one of Tillingfold's traditional enemies, had piled up a hundred and forty-three runs for Raveley – the highest score ever made against the village. Four balls passed his bat all afternoon. Deacon had counted them. When eventually the batsman lifted a gentle little lob off the edge of the bat, looping back over his head straight to the keeper, Deacon was so mesmerised his feet would not take the one step forward he needed to make the catch; and the ball dropped quietly to earth a yard in front of him. 'Fuck!' was torn from his lips and he flung both his gloves to the ground, narrowly stopping himself from stamping on them. 'That's enough of that!' Gauvinier's voice was steel behind him. 'Pick 'em up and get on with the game.'

Deacon could feel the skipper's eyes boring into his spine as he crouched, suddenly wide awake again behind the stumps. That was all that had been said, but Deacon had never again sworn out loud on the field. Like young White, he valued his place in the Tillingfold team beyond most things: even beyond a peaceful home life, if the truth be known.

Archibald, the Wym batsman, wondered how on earth he'd not been given out and glad even if slightly guilty that he hadn't 'walked'. He'd heard the click as the ball went through his hasty defensive prod but did not know, as the umpire did, that the noise came from the ball flicking the top of his pad as he jumped back from its trajectory. Defiantly he took guard again, restoring his fluttering nerves, and hit the second ball, a fast full toss, for four. As a shot it wasn't much, but off a thick edge the ball streaked away to the boundary past Gillian's left hand at gully with not a finger laid on it. She had plenty of time on the trek to retrieve it to wonder whether to be grateful the ball had whistled past her too far away to reach, or to be ashamed of herself that she hadn't at least tried to dive for it. But then it was early in the game and one just hadn't had time to warm up yet, she excused herself, tossing the ball back to the bowler with a subdued 'Sorry, Norman.'

Her discomfiture was by no means improved by a sardonic voice from cover: 'Girls – couldn't catch a bloody fly.' Which was no less wounding even though the ball had passed her all along the ground. 'Cut it out, Paul,' Gauvinier said sharply, wondering instantly whether he was being too protective and kicking himself mentally.

The third ball, short and fast and coming through outside the off stump at stump height, Archibald met with a full and free swing of the bat – a genuine square cut, and sent the ball hard towards cover point, straight at White. That worthy, loped forward confidently to pick it up one-handed, but the ball, travelling very fast, skipped suddenly off a bump in the outfield, delivered him a painful blow on the wrist and ran through to the boundary. White, furious, turned to pick it up and jerk it back to the wicketkeeper, his temper in no way improved by Jess's cheerful jeer. 'Two hands, then, Paulie.' And Gillian was glad she hadn't uttered them although they were on her lips as well as on those of several others on the ground.

'Bad luck, Paul,' called Gauvinier. 'That one jumped.' And White, rubbing his wrist ruefully, could do no more than call, 'Sorry Norman,' just as Gillian had done half a minute before.

Smith's fourth ball, on a good length outside the off stump, the batsman was happy to leave alone and

Deacon, taking it a little carelessly in front of his body, fumbled and dropped it onto his left foot, whereupon it rolled a few yards away to leg and the batsmen scrambled a quick run. 'Damn,' thought Deacon as he scuttled after the ball, automatically dropping his right glove lest a quick throw should be needed. 'Damn.' And he made up his mind to dismiss all thoughts of Gina from the Lancing Road, at least until he was safely back in the pavilion.

Fanshawe, leaning awkwardly on his shooting stick, signalled the bye with his right forefinger above his head, and from the scorers' window in the pavilion a hand waved acknowledgement. Wym's second opening batsman, a thin, dark man with an intense expression, called officiously, 'Centre, a shade to leg, if you please Mr Umpire.' And Fanshawe, an authoritarian who disliked other authoritarians, stifled a wish to see Norman Smith's sixth ball knock out his middle stump.

Alas for such wishes. The thin, intense man hit the last ball of Norman's over, a straight half-volley, clean over the bowler's head for six. It was a free, beautifully timed strike that was as unexpected as it was fluent. As the home side broke into ragged cheers from the pavilion, the bowler stood with hands on hips staring at the batsman with astonishment. No fast bowler likes to be hit straight back over his head, and it was unique in Norman's experience for any batsman in any class of cricket to do so off the first ball of his innings. It just had to be a fluke. He turned round to grab the ball as Jess returned it from far outside the field of play, forgetting he had finished his over, so intent was he on getting his revenge. 'You wait,' he said to himself. 'You bloody wait.' But like the rest of the Tillingfold side, Norman had applauded the shot spontaneously as the ball flew high over their heads and over the boundary fence. 'Forty yards,' called Jess, tossing it back after a vault over the barbed wire and long trot through the sheep; meaning that the ball had pitched forty yards outside the playing area, a full hundred yards from the popping crease. At Lord's it would have threatened the sleeping members on the second tier of the pavilion. Here at Wym, the only beings in danger were the sheep, and they paid little attention.

Fifteen runs off the over, and an unsuccessful appeal. Quite an eventful start, thought Gauvinier as he handed the ball to Hunter to try his luck at the other end.

It was a ploy he'd often used with success, for although there were at least three better bowlers in the team than Frank Hunter, the shock of being faced with a slow leg-spinner had undone more than one village team in the past. Most opening batsmen are quite prepared to suffer a knock or two from the fast bowlers; it's what they expect, and many a batsman will tell you that the faster the ball comes onto the bat the faster it goes off it. Gauvinier often wondered about the mythology of the first-class game, where for fifteen years slow bowlers had been almost eliminated in favour of a dreary succession of medium-fast seamers on the quite spurious grounds that 'they keep the runs down'. Anyway, he cherished the day when an Old Boys side from a famous public school had arrived to play Tillingfold on a dank wet afternoon and their opening batsmen had turned out sporting defensive helmets. 'I ask you,' he'd said to Fanshawe afterwards. He'd put Frank Hunter on one end and Fred Bason on the other, slow leg-spin and slow off-spin respectively, they'd taken four wickets apiece and Tillingfold had won their first ever game against a touring side by six o'clock in the evening. Tillingfold had quite an evening in the Dog and Duck that night, none the whit spoilt by the fact that the Old Boys, smarting with the disgrace, whacked the home side out of sight at both darts and skittles, and had to be poured into their coach long after closing time.

At Wym, however, the ploy did not work. To be honest, a phrase Frank used quite often in both his business dealings and his everyday speech, he didn't really like opening the bowling, honour though he felt it to be. Consoling himself that he could always blame the skipper in the pub afterwards, Hunter bowled two full tosses and four long-hops, and was fortunate not to give away more than one three and three fours, the latter to the dark intense batsman, encouraged by an increasing chorus of support from the pavilion.

'Come on Bruce! Give 'em stick! Good old Bruce!'

Bruce glanced towards the pavilion with no change to his sardonic expression, and proceeded, as the cricket saying goes, to take the Tillingfold attack apart. Hunter, after conceding twenty-eight runs in his first two overs and a further twenty in his third (three giant sixes from Bruce) was taken off and sent into the outfield to nurse his bruised pride. Norman Smith, settling down to a good length, was not so expensive, and indeed counted himself unlucky when twice good balls moved off the pitch to beat both bat and wicket; and a third time when a snicked drive from Archibald flew at catchable height between Gauvinier and Gillian, through the space vacated by Hunter at second slip. But he too conceded six runs an over, one way or another, and the score was sixty-six for no wickets after only seven overs when Gauvinier took Hunter's place to bowl.

At his best Gauvinier, like his father, could be a subtle and deceptive left-arm seamer. He did not bowl fast, but achieved a pace off the pitch which often caught even experienced batsmen unawares. Today he rather fancied his chances on the mottled Wym pitch, particularly against a hitter like Bruce. His first ball was driven ferociously back down the pitch at him, and he got a hand to it, taking the force off the stroke but bruising his fingers. The second went through the air humming like a top, and Mitterman prudently made no attempt to stop it as it kicked viciously a couple of yards in front of him and leapt past his face on its way to the square-leg boundary. The third rattled the wooden wall of the pavilion, the fourth and fifth were straight-driven with awesome power for four – and the sixth was despatched contemptuously, as befitted a slow full-toss, for six, again over square-leg's head.

Gauvinier had never known an over like it since he had been hit, as a colt some thirty-five years before, for five sixes in one over. He did recall, too, the last over before lunch at Southend in 1948, when Bradman hit Frank Vigar of Essex for five consecutive fours. Today at Wym the Tillingfold fielders displayed much the same impotent immobility as the men of Essex had that day so long ago. However, twenty-two in one over did impressive things for Wym's morale, and eighty-eight for no wickets was beginning to look ominous for Tillingfold. Gauvinier, crossing his mental fingers and sending up a silent prayer that her morale would not be shattered for life, tossed the ball to Gillian. 'Time to tame them, Gill. Give it a try from Norman's end.'

Miss Grantham was not at all sure she wanted the ball. For all her sturdy independence, the utter ferocity of Bruce's hitting was intimidating. Wym was a long way from Loughborough. However, Mr Bruce would not be her immediate antagonist at the crease. His co-opener, Mr Archibald, would be facing up to her first ball, and he looked much the simpler proposition of the two. His pink cheeks, fair hair and blue eyes had had several young ladies in a state of considerable agitation at Fenners on a number of occasions, though not, it must be said, when the University was in action, for Clive Archibald had been an intermittent member of his college Second XI, and as such of course knew a great deal more about the game than any number of experts. Gillian had classified him mentally on sight as an Old Non-Blue, a type she'd met many times both at Loughborough and since, and she fancied she knew exactly what was going through his mind as she paced out her run.

Archibald, indeed, was making his attitude pretty clear. As a good and faithful member of the Gloucestershire Young Farmers Association, and vice-chairman of the Wym Young Conservatives, he waxed mortally indignant at any suggestion of male chauvinism. And yet, a girl playing cricket! This Tillingfold side must be short. He stood at the popping crease, bat hanging loosely in his hand. No need to take fresh guard, thank you, Mr Umpire. Right arm over? Well, at least she doesn't bowl underarm. Hmm . . . not a bad looker, either. Wonder if she . . . Oh-oh, here she comes. Let's see how far I can belt this one. Bound to be a dolly . . .

Afterwards he swore it was the wicket. The ball, faster than he expected, pitched short of a length and rose a little. Archibald, determined to thrash it out of the ground (he'd been smarting a bit at the successes of Bruce at the other end), swung cross-batted with all his force. The ball careered of the top edge full into his face and thence in a gentle parabola to Hunter in the gully. 'HOWZATT!' half a dozen Tillingfold pairs of hands lifted in triumph. Archibald, half stunned by the blow to his cheekbone, staggered back, dropped his bat, fell over the wicket and collapsed to the ground in front of Deacon, both hands clutched to his face. He lay and moaned gently to himself as the fielders clustered round, joined more slowly by Bruce. There wasn't much love lost between the Wym opening batsmen.

Bruce edged through the fielders and, not ungently, parted the clutching hands. Archibald's left eye was beginning to swell. The angry bruise on his cheek was split at the centre, and a fair amount of blood had found its way onto his batting gloves and had blotched around his face. The sight was not pretty, but there was more blood than guts, as White said later.

'Come on, you'll be all right.' Bruce helped him to his feet and picked up his bat. There was a subdued clap from the pavilion.

'Bad luck, batsman,' said Gauvinier, who had read the little pantomime before the ball was delivered with some amusement. 'And by the way, you're out. You can get that fixed in the pavilion.'

Archibald stared at him from his good eye. He remembered the ball coming towards him. Nothing after that.

'What . . . what happened?'

'You were either caught or hit wicket,' said Gauvinier. The Wym umpire was still making good the broken wicket to his full satisfaction. 'We appealed, both umpires put their hands up. So I reckon you're out, twice.'

'On your way, Archie.' The taciturn Bruce was

impatient. 'You're holding up the game.'

Archibald walked off disconsolately, nursing his wounded cheek along with his injured pride, and not at all mollified by the sceptical questioning of his teammates and the scorers who, it seemed, wanted to know how he had been (a) laid flat by a girl and (b) dismissed. He ignored Budgeon's cheerful 'Bad luck. How were you out?' and disappeared head-down into the little dressing room.

'It's all very well,' grumbled Budgeon to his Wym colleague, a little hunchback with a bright bird-like eye, 'but you have to know what to put down.' And under the 'How Out' column he wrote, in pencil 'c Hunter / Ht Wkt b Grantham.'

The hunchback, argumentatively as he considered Wym well on top, opined that, 'It must be caught; he hit the ball and was caught.'

And Budgeon, not to be put down, replied: 'Ah, but he broke the wicket making the stroke. Any road, I wish t'had been t'other one gone.'

'Ah, Bruce. Strange man, Bruce. Strange man.' And he did not elucidate further, obviously believing that a sage nod of the head and a meaningful look were explanation enough for an outsider. Which of course Budgeon respected, being a villager himself and the Tillingfold cobbler. So he merely commented, 'Good batsman, though.' And marked down a dot against Gillian Grantham's name in the scorebook, denoting a ball from which no runs were scored. His companion swelled visibly.

'One of the best in the county,' commented the Wym scorer, marking down two runs for the next batsman, Skinner, for a neat push to leg. 'Should've played for Somerset you know, but they couldn't take him at

Taunton. Look at this.'

And he turned back the scorebook to show how William Bruce had scored a hundred and two, including nine sixes and ten fours, in a Gloucestershire second league match a month before. 'In thirty-five minutes, too. Should be in the Guinness Book of Records, that score, I reckon.'

'Hope he doesn't do it today,' grunted Budgeon. 'Oh-oh. I don't think he's going to . . .' He leaned forward out of the scorer's window to follow the flight of the ball. Bruce had taken a stride forward to a ball that Gauvinier held back a little, and which dipped and pitched slightly shorter than he had expected. The ball, instead of sailing cleanly over Gauvinier's head for six, was climbing almost vertically, hanging at the top of its parabola and dropping straight into the hands of Edgar Trine at deep long on. He judged it perfectly, watching it all the way down into his hands, palms held out in front of his face in the Australian manner. 'Well . . .' The Tillingfold congratulations died in their throats as the ball, inexplicably, popped out of the cupped hands and ran gently through Trine's legs to the boundary.

'Butterfingered lot, your side,' the Wym scorer said, adding four to Bruce's score. 'Well,' totting up the score with the rubber end of his pencil, 'I make that sixty-eight. Only thirty-two to go for his ton. D'you agree?'

'Hang on a bit, I'm not so quick as you.' Figures were not Budgeon's long suit. 'Yes, that's about right . . . that young chap doesn't usually miss a sitter like that.'

'A pretty high one,' said the Wym scorer magnanimously, but Budgeon was in no mood to accept the olive branch. The young chap in question meanwhile was sucking his fingers and wondering how the devil he'd come to drop a catch like that. Straight into his hands. And with that damned girl looking on, too. He tossed the ball back first bounce to Gauvinier.

'Sorry, Guv.'

'Never mind, Teddy. It was a pretty high one.'

Gauvinier tried to hide his disappointment without much success. Every bowler who has a catch downed has a right to feel aggrieved. He had schemed for that wicket, studying the batsman, deliberately feeding his strength to deceive him into making the false stroke, and watched his efforts dribble out of young Trine's hands over the boundary for another four.

'Lucky beggar,' he thought. He wondered whether the let-off would make the batsman more cautious, or if, like some he had known (even like himself on occasion), the chap would conclude his luck was in and go for his shots even more boldly, if that were possible. Gauvinier discarded 'Lightning never strikes twice' for 'Why not?' and delivered exactly the same ball again, but this time from a yard further back, his front foot on the bowling crease, not well in front of it. The effect was spectacular. Seeing a similar ball floating temptingly towards him, Bruce stepped down the wicket again, left and right foot shuffle, and swung mightily. Once again the ball soared into the air in the direction of the deep long on. Trine, gazing up into the blue, had no thought for his previous miss. He watched it carefully, moved back a pace or two, looked round quickly to check he was not leaning on the boundary fence, and caught the ball two handed above and behind his head, his back arched like a bow so as not to touch the fence and so give away a six. White might have made it; Jess ten years ago and Gauvinier twenty, but no one else on the side. The field rang to genuine applause for a magnificent piece of cricket. Bruce, who hadn't even bothered to run for the hit, thinking it was a six all the way, thumped his bat on the ground, muttered 'I'll be buggered!' and strode off angrily to the pavilion, forgetting how he had been dropped off the previous ball.

As the fielders clustered round Trine, slapping him on the back, examining his fingers and ribbing him about the dropped catch – it was safe to do that now – Fanshawe carefully transferred another stone from pocket to pocket and said quietly to Gauvinier, 'Well bowled, Peter.'

'Thanks.' He felt a deep satisfaction that he had been able both to read a situation and rise to it, that this time Trine hadn't let him down, had in fact surpassed himself, and that the danger man had been removed at long last. He checked the scoreboard. Ninety-two, two, sixty-eight it read, and he realised there was plenty more work to be done.

'Come on everyone, man in,' he called. He had to remember not to call 'chaps' which was his usual habit, now that Gillian was in the team. His clap of the hands was louder than usual, nominally to welcome the new batsman, more particularly to shake Tillingfold out of any complacency they might feel having broken a long stand. Gauvinier knew that there was still a long way to go. Tillingfold weren't on top yet. A point which was proved when Brown, the Wym skipper and next man in, hit his first ball from Gauvinier for four, a nicely timed drive all along the ground and beating Jess's desperate scramble to cut it off short of the boundary. Gauvinier was thankful it was the end of the over. He liked to study a batsman for a few balls before bowling to him.

He tossed the ball to Gillian, and strolled across to

Norman Smith. He didn't want to let the young man think a good spell of bowling had passed unnoticed.

'I'll give Gillian a few overs, then perhaps you'll have better luck in your second spell,' he said as they crossed over.

'Ok, Guv.' But Smith was none too pleased, with himself as with the situation, and, like many young men, he was still learning to ascribe the causes of misfortune to something within himself, and not to outside circumstances. Just at the moment, he was blaming the wicket, the journey, the lunchtime pint and even the warm sunshine for his lack of success, whereas in reality, perhaps, he was trying just that bit too hard, trying to bowl just that much too fast, or to impart just too much swerve onto an obstinate ball that refused to obey.

Perhaps it was his preoccupation with his own performance that brought about even more frustration for young Norman. During Gillian's next over, Brown, as agricultural in stance as in appearance, produced what could only be described as a mow. It was a perfectly adequate shot, he felt, which had brought him any number of runs in the past; but this time, instead of running swiftly along the ground, the ball flew in a high fierce parabola towards Smith at deep fine leg, or long leg, as the commentators say these days. Norman, usually a safe fielder, positioned himself for the catch, and, at the last moment, saw the ball was dipping more sharply than he expected. He took a hesitant step forward, then two back as the trajectory seemed to flatten out like that of a glider. Brown, the batsman, paused in his run to watch the awful inevitability (to him) of the catch, only to see the fieldsman lunge forward desperately at the last moment, clutching the ball with both hands only for it to pop up twice like a piece of wet soap as Norman grabbed for it, and fall innocuously to the ground. Hardly able to contain himself, he leapt after the offending object and hurled it with all his force in the vague direction of the wicketkeeper. Norman was a powerful young man, and the ball sped with a rising trajectory six feet over Deacon's gloves at the wicket and, evading the combined efforts of Jess and White on the other side of the field, crossed the boundary for four overthrows, giving Brown the striker a very handy bonus in the scorebook.

'Five,' muttered Budgeon in disgust. 'And to think he dropped a sitter.'

To which the Wym scorer, on top of the world as nothing seemed to go wrong for his team, piled Pelion on Ossa. 'Caught twice, dropped three times,' he said, and Budgeon had to press hard on his ballpoint pen to hold back a cutting, but no doubt equally fatuous, retort. But his feelings were reflected through the Tillingfold team on the field, where Gauvinier fancied he could see shoulders droop at the double mishap.

'And I had him. Sure of it,' Deacon muttered audibly, referring to the fact that the Wym batsman had been well out of his crease when Norman's throw-in passed over his head like a swallow.

'Never mind, lads,' Gauvinier's voice was sharp. 'Let's tighten up now.' And Gillian, the bowler, not noticing his slip, clenched her teeth and delivered five very good balls indeed, beating the bat three times and drawing the batsman forward with the last one. Deacon had the bails off in a flash, his 'HAAAT!' shattering the afternoon simultaneously, and enlarged to a roar by Fred Bason and Frank Hunter, both standing fairly square of the wicket.

The batsman, who had slid his foot back into the crease almost at the same time, stood his ground.

'Not out,' said the Wym umpire at square leg. And Deacon's face turned an unhealthy puce, not mollified by Gauvinier's hasty 'Bad luck, good try.'

'I bloody well know when I've bloody well stumped a bugger,' he muttered to himself. And indeed he did. He had watched the ball from the moment it left Gillian's hand, seen the curve into the bat, the break off the seam beating the reaching stoke, and the right foot slide forward over the line, pushing back a fraction after he had whipped the bails off with a classic flick of the gloves.

He stumped up the wicket to commiserate with Gillian, 'Bloody good ball, that. We had the bugger,' clapping her on the back, and not noticing that they were just two cricketers together. 'Their bloody umpire.'

Gillian said vehemently: 'That was the best ball I've bowled all day,' not noticing either that Joe Deacon had not actually said 'bloody' or 'bugger' but used the famous four-letter word not meant to be spoken in the presence of a lady. In harmonious resentment they took their places for Gauvinier's next over.

Gauvinier hoped that the Wym side would show some signs of frailty after the dismissal of their big hitter. But Brown's new partner sported a faded Harlequin's cap and a cravat tucked into a cream silk shirt, took guard with a quick tap of the bat in the blockhole, and cut Gauvinier's first ball wristily for two comfortable runs. No easy pickings here, thought Gauvinier as he prepared to bowl the next ball, only to be stopped in his stride as the batsman stepped back from the wicket and held up a gloved hand. Then he advanced down the pitch waving his bat angrily. Gauvinier turned to see in the field behind him a pony trap driven at a languid trot heading toward the field of play.

'Sorry, bowler,' said the batsman in an aside to Gauvinier. 'Stupid bloody woman. She never learns,' waving his bat furiously all the while. The driver of the trap, suddenly conscious of the fact that she was holding up play, turned her horse's head away from the line of the wicket and began to trot round the perimeter fence. 'I keep telling her, but it makes no difference.' And he stumped back down the wicket to take his guard all over again, his middle-aged face gradually returning from its shade of puce to its jollier ruddiness.

'Her ladyship doesn't understand cricket,' Brown whispered to Gauvinier while all this was going on, from which Gauvinier understood that the batsman facing him was Lord Wym. 'She makes him hopping mad,' said Brown, and Gauvinier, thinking to tempt the irate peer into an indiscretion, put down a slow half-volley on the leg stump which Lord Wym, with a non-aristocractic swipe, belted over the square leg boundary for four runs, narrowly missing the pony trap and causing the horse to shy.

'Hundred up,' said the Wym scorer, and one of the watching players rose languidly to his feet to amend the scoreboard. 'His lordship's in form today. Phew. It's getting warm in here.' And he fanned himself with his scorebook.

Out on the field, Tillingfold sweated and strained, but it was one of those days, as Bason said later, when nothing seemed to go right. After her early success, Gillian had bowled well but with no luck at all, while Gauvinier, try as he might, failed to rediscover the touch which had enabled him to tempt the leading batsman to offer up two catches off successive balls. Gauvinier tried a double change of bowling: Smith for himself and Fred Bason for Gillian. It made no difference. The contrasting styles of the batsmen seemed a foil for the best the Tillingfold bowlers could produce. The Earl of Wym, who indeed had played for Cambridge in his youth, was still in his mid fifties a neat, forceful batsman. Brown, the skipper, had no pretensions to batsmanship, but his stiff-armed approach was backed by a good eye and, on this occasion at least, a great deal of luck. The score mounted steadily. The batsmen took it past the hundred and fifty mark, and Gauvinier, looking at his watch, wondered just how many they would put on before the tea interval. One good thing about village cricket was that neither side could go on too long, he thought. But the Tillingfold fielding was beginning to wilt under the hot sun and the double-fisted attack of the batsmen. Gauvinier looked up at the blue sky and, finding no inspiration there, decided to keep Norman Smith on for one more over.

The young man had bowled a second excellent spell, with just as little success as in his first few overs. Several times he had beaten the bat outside the off stump, without getting a touch. Brown had scored three fours off the inside edge and the Earl had narrowly avoided being caught by Frank Hunter in the slips – a diving chance that left that worthy sucking the end of his fingers. 'Try one more, Norman,' Gauvinier called, and young Smith determined that this time he would take a wicket or burst in the attempt.

He added a couple of paces to his run-up for luck and stormed in to deliver the fastest ball in his repertoire.

Afterwards he could not explain why, but in the delivery stride he changed his mind completely. Instead of the threatened all-out attack, the Earl of Wym found himself facing a slow, high, gentle full-toss, as inviting a ball as ever lured a batsman to his doom. The Earl, instead of placing his stroke competently between the fielders for a certain four, flailed wildly at the ball as it hovered somewhere above his off stump, missed completely and was aghast to see it drop, almost in slow motion, full pitch into the bails. He stared at the shattered wicket in disbelief, swore under his breath, grinned, and marched off with his bat under his arm.

'A hundred and eighty-five, three, thirty-nine.' The Wym scorer dropped his pencil to applaud the Earl into the pavilion. 'Brown's got forty-six. Add a couple of extras and you've got a stand of ninety. Pity they didn't put the hundred up.' But Budgeon, who was growing hot and irritated, had had enough of his partner's cockiness and refused to be drawn.

'Well bowled, Norman.'

'You lucky son of a gun.'

'Where'd you get that one from?'

The fieldsmen clustered around Smith, relieved at the ending of a long stand.

'Aw, it was just a bit of luck, he said awkwardly, which indeed it was, but as Fred Bason said in his slow way, 'Ah, but 'twas a darned good idea, toss him one up like that.'

'He should have hit it into next week,' said Trine cheerfully, 'but he didn't. Come on chaps, let's get this over.' For he, like the others, had had enough running about in the hot sun.

So had Norman, and he produced a beauty next ball, the ball pitching dead on the middle stump and knocking the leg stump out of the ground, having passed the batsman's defensive prod as though there was no bat at all.

'That's more like it.' Gauvinier called in all his troops. 'Let's go for the hat-trick.'

There is nothing like a couple of quick wickets to put life into a flagging fielding side. Tillingfold gathered round the incoming batsman, stretching out eager hands for the catch they felt sure would come. Even Mitterman responded to the urgency of the moment, moving a few yards closer to the batsman, who eyed all these preparations with a mixture of misgiving and defiance. He knew full well he was 'on a hat-trick', as they say in cricket, and he wasn't sure whether to try to block with a straight bat, as he had been urged in the pavilion, or to hit his way out of trouble. Being a cheerful lad, and a computer programmer to boot, he decided to throw science to the winds and as the ball hurtled towards him he took an almighty heave. The ball flew straight at Mitterman who, standing only six yards from the bat, had no time to duck or move out of the way. With a despairing gesture he flung up both hands to save his life, but not quickly enough. The ball struck him a painful blow on the left shoulder and bounded high in the air. Jess, yelling 'I've got it' so loudly his voice cracked, sprinted in to take the catch as Mitterman, unaware and unmindful of the whereabouts of the ball, collapsed in a heap on the ground, rubbing his shoulder furiously.

The bowler, whose feelings had soared, plummeted and soared again in approximately a second and a half, ran over to shake Jess by the hand. 'You caught it, Albert. You caught it,' he kept repeating. It was only the second hat-trick of his career. He went over to Mitterman, still sitting on the ground rubbing his shoulder. 'Well fielded, James,' he said with no sense of irony.

Mitterman looked at him sourly, rubbing at his shoulder. 'I didn't want to stop the bloody thing,' he said. But nothing could dim Norman's happiness. It was a moment he would tell to his grandchildren, and no amount of sour grapes from Mitterman was going to spoil his moment of triumph.

Brown wasn't the sort of cricketer to let the grass grow under his feet, and besides, he wanted his fifty. So the batsmen had crossed during the alarums and excursions of Norman's hat-trick wicket. But Norman had found a new lease of life and Brown found himself desperately defending his wicket for the last three balls of the over. The last he sliced heavily into the covers and set off for what seemed a safe, if brisk run. But White swooped right-handed to the ball, picking it up cleanly and whipping it back towards the wicket with a professional underarm flick of the wrist. Brown hesitated fatally, and dived for the crease, sending up a cloud of dust and grass seed and heavily staining his pads which had been especially whited for the occasion. But all his effort was in vain, for Norman had caught the stinging ball cleanly and broken the wicket, and Brown was run out, his groping bat still six inches outside the crease.

'It just shows you. You can never tell about cricket.' Gauvinier felt that rarely had his favourite maxim been more clearly demonstrated. From a hundred and eighty-five for two wickets, the home side had progressed to a hundred and eighty-five for six in the course of just one over; and the turn-around in fortunes was complete when, on the stroke of five o'clock, Gauvinier himself bowled the last batsman and Wym were all out for a hundred and ninety-nine. Norman Smith was rewarded for his marathon efforts with six wickets, albeit for ninety runs.

'Not too bad,' Gauvinier told his weary team as they trooped into the pavilion together. 'It looked as though we might be facing nearer three hundred at one time. Until Norman got his act together.' And they stood back to let the hat-trick taker into the pavilion first, generously applauded by the home side who had lined up outside the little building.

'Bad luck, skipper,' he said to Brown. To be out four short of your fifty was bad enough, but to run yourself out into the bargain was rubbing salt into your own wound.

'It was my own fault,' Brown acknowledged. 'But that young fielder of yours was pretty good. So's your bowler.' He paused. 'And your young lady. She surprised me, I'm bound to admit.'

'Oh, Gillian's surprised quite a few people this summer.' He told Brown how she had come to join the club. Brown laughed.

'Anyway, come and have some tea,' he said.

Normally, the Wym tea was served in the pavilion. Today, in deference to the weather, the trestle tables had been carried out under the big beech tree alongside the pavilion. They made a cheerful sight.

'Thirsty work out there.' Lord Wym poured out a glass of orange juice from a big blue and white earthenware jug and handed it to Gauvinier. He drank greedily.

'I needed that.'

'Help yourself to sandwiches. Don't be shy. There's plenty for everyone.'

The players clustered round the tables like flies. Indeed there was plenty: thick white home-made bread sandwiches with good butter and wedges of the local cheese; two big dishes full of ripe tomatoes; and two home-made fruit cakes already cut into slices.

'If that's as good as it looks . . .'

'What's this cheese?'

'Oh, that's Double Gloucester. They make it in the village . . .'

'D'you grow your own tomatoes?'

'Good idea, this orange juice . . .'

'What's a nice girl like you doing playing a rough game like cricket?'

Gillian Grantham was quite accustomed to this type of approach. She ignored it and looked the young blond man up and down. The bruise on his cheek was somewhat subdued by a large piece of sticking-plaster, and his left eye was beginning to show a delicate shade of purple.

'Does it hurt much?' She wasn't too sympathetic.

'Oh, not too bad.' He lifted a cautious hand and touched the sticking plaster gingerly. 'You might have told me you could bowl.'

'It had nothing to do with the ball. That was a lousy shot.'

'Yes, but girls aren't supposed to know about things like that.'

'Why ever not?'

'Yes, why not?' The rough Sussex voice sounded truculent. Gillian raised her eyebrows. The last champion she had expected was Paul White.

'Oh, no reason at all.' The young Wym batsman was apologetic. 'It's just that it's the first time I've actually met a lady cricketer.'

White was unmollified. But his truculence was mitigated by the fact that he found it difficult to articulate through a mouthful of bread, cheese and tomato. He contented himself with a threatening grunt and moved off to swill down his food with a mug of tea.

'He doesn't approve of me either,' Gillian said to Archibald. 'It's just that I'm one of us, as it were, and you're one of them.'

'Seriously, though, haven't you found it embarrassing, being a girl cricketer?'

'I'm not half as embarrassed as some of the men.' Gillian laughed. 'But they've got used to me, I think.'

Lord Wym moved into the conversation with the easy authority of a man used to exercising his *droit de seigneur*.

'Oh, Archibald. Do nip over and give Robert a hand with the roller, there's a good chap.' He laid a hand on Gillian's arm. 'Your skipper has been telling me about you. You're quite a girl, aren't you?' His hand squeezed her arm. Gillian disengaged it on the pretext of picking up a mug of tea. His lordship proferred the sugar with one hand, neatly sliding his other arm round her waist. Gillian looked at him. She knew several remedies to situations like this. She quite enjoyed the delay while she made her choice. Lord Wym received the cup of tea neatly on the navel, soaking him from the waist down and sending tea-coloured streaks coursing down his flannels.

'Oh dear,' said Gillian with patent insincerity. 'It must have slipped. So sorry.'

She left the Earl mopping vainly at the front of his flannels with a silk handkerchief and grinning wryly to himself. He liked a girl with spirit.

'Gillian, my love, that wasn't very polite to our host.'

Trine had watched the incident with amusement. 'You might at least have helped dry him down.' She liked Trine. In his easy way, he had always been an ally.

'It was a bit drastic, I admit. But what would you do if a middle-aged wolf started pawing at you? Lie back and think of England?'

'Well, in my case one would hope it would be a wolverine. But I see what you mean. And then, I'd rather think of Sweden.' Trine's penchant for Swedish au pair girls was standard Tillingfold gossip, which he did nothing to discourage.

Bason was talking to the sour-faced Bruce, who turned out to be Wym's shopkeeper and postmaster. He asked if it was difficult to make a living in a small village like Wym. Belying his appearance, Bruce took quite a cheerful outlook on life.

'It's not so bad out here. We're more than fifteen miles from Bristol, see, so most of the old folks come to me.' He couldn't match the prices of the supermarkets in the towns, but had joined one of the organisations which catered for small shops and, after all, he said, 'It costs them petrol to drive to Sainsbury's or Tesco's. So its six to one and half a dozen to the other.'

'Holding the post office licence helps, doesn't it?' Bason, in his younger days, had been Tillingfold's postmaster.

'It's all right,' Bruce said without enthusiasm. 'I suppose I'd miss it if they took it away.'

'You cagey old blighter. It's your life's blood and you know it.' The speaker was the youngest member of the Wym side, a curly-headed youth with something of Trine's easy manner. 'Tell him about the time when you defended it with your life.'

'Oh come on, Master Wym, that's all water under the bridge.'

'What happened?' asked Bason, intrigued. And ignoring Bruce's protests, Rupert Wym obliged.

'It must have been a couple of years ago. There was a spate of small post office robberies at the time. Anyway, Norman here had seen this chap in the village a couple of days before and hadn't liked the look of him. Apparently the bloke must have been casing the joint because in some way he'd fixed the burglar alarm so it didn't go off. The first Norman heard – he sleeps over the shop, of course – was someone moving around downstairs. So he switches on all the lights and goes down and there's this chap holding a gun and telling him to get the keys of the safe. So Norman hits him over the wrist with his cricket bat and breaks his arm and then lets him have one in the knee and one over the head just to keep him quiet, and then he rings up Ted the policeman and asks him to come round and collect a package.'

'What happened to him?'

'Oh, it turned out that he'd a record as long as your arm – a robbery with violence, gbh, and the rest. He got five years and Norm here got a commendation from the court and £25 reward from the grateful Post Office.'

Bason raised an eyebrow at Bruce. 'True?' he said. Bruce permitted himself a thin smile.

'That's enough of that,' was all he would say, and refused to be pressed farther.

'Where'd you learn your cricket?' Bason asked him.

'Sri Lanka,' was the surprising answer. 'Although they called it Ceylon then. I was born out there . . .' Bason recalled the wiry freedom of Bruce's hitting and compared it with what he'd seen of the little known Sri

Lankans on television. There was certainly a similarity but there was not time to pursue the conversation now, as someone rang a bell in the pavilion and Brown began chivvying the Wym team onto the field before even Fanshawe had completed his second cup of tea.

Chapter Four

A TARGET OF TWO HUNDRED is asking a great deal from a village cricket club, and Gauvinier spent most of the tea interval pondering his batting order. On their day several of his batsmen were capable of making runs – even a fifty – but he had experienced too many disastrous Tillingfold collapses to be at all sanguine about the outcome of the match. In any case, although Wym had scored their runs at a fair rate – well over a run a minute – Tillingfold would have less time to bid for the total. The Wym innings had lasted a fraction under 2½ hours. Tillingfold would have (always assuming they didn't collapse) from 5.25 to 7.30 to score the runs, although under the modern rule it was actually 'twenty overs from 6.30'. It was another of those regulations which had filtered down from the first-class game designed to speed things up, and Gauvinier detested it. He far preferred to time matters by Tillingfold's church clock chiming the quarters, or by his watch at away fixtures not blessed with a clock. He had rarely found that a village side dawdled their way through the overs, even though there might be some famous stonewallers among the batsmen. Tillingfold's answer to deliberate go-slow tactics was merely to terminate the fixture. And as Tillingfold teas were famous all over Sussex, few clubs wanted to risk the wrath of the fixtures secretary. Mitterman could write a mean letter when he put his mind to it.

Gauvinier always had a problem with Mitterman. He had made himself too useful to the club to drop from the team; but he didn't bowl ('thank the Lord for that' was Gauvinier's heartfelt comment), was but a poor field and an unreliable batsman at best. However, 'He looks the part,' Gauvinier had often said to Fanshawe, excusing himself, and putting Mitterman down to open the batting. And indeed, Mitterman's immaculate appearance did make an impression upon new opponents. But today was different. 'James,' he said diplomatically, 'we want to pile on the runs a bit and it's not quite your style. We're going to need a bit of solidity in the middle order. Six or seven do?'

Mitterman nodded. He wanted to run over the arrangements for the team's overnight stay and to chivvy up the last of the late payers. At least he did not have to bully the team for the tea money. In recognition of Tillingfold's long journey, Brown had waived the customary 50p a head from the visitors. 'You can buy the beer afterwards,' he grinned as he poked his head round the door of the busy dressing room.

'Just like a skipper. Gets himself out to save paying for a jug,' someone said. It was good to hear the lingua franca of cricket breaking the ice between the teams.

Brown laughed: 'No such luck. Here they'll fine me a jug instead. See you later.'

Gauvinier made up his mind. It had to be all-out attack, he felt.

'Albert, will you open, please? And Paul, get your pads on as well if you don't mind. I'll take first down, Trine number four, Frank five, Fred six, you, James, seven, Gillian eight, Norman nine, Richard ten and Joe props us all up. Okay?' He completed his list and took it out for the scorers to fill into their books. He noticed the umpires already at the wicket and the fieldsmen beginning to take their positions, and hurried back to the dressing room.

'Come on, chaps, they're waiting.' He paused. 'We haven't all that much time, but get a good look at the bowling before you go mad, Paul.' He had no need to caution Jess, an old hand at the game, but young White's natural arrogance always needed reining in. Still, they looked a competent enough pair of cricketers on their way to the wicket, and Gauvinier hastened to pad up so he would be able to watch the first ball bowled. He did not usually bat so high in the order himself, but he felt it incumbent on him to lead from the front, if indeed he could.

'Gar,' said the little Wym scorer to Budgeon. 'Is that *the* Albert Jess? The pop star?'

'Mmmm.' Tillingfold had grown accustomed to Jess, whose star days in any case were several years past. 'He teaches the church choir, too.'

'Gar,' said the little scorer, unbelieving.

'S'true.' And indeed it was. Some years before, when Jess had shed his illusions with the jet-set scene and come home rich to Tillingfold, where he had been born, he discovered that the choirmistress had just died, and the vicar, the Reverend Veysey, had no musical ability – in fact he was tone deaf. He had struck a bargain with the vicar, part of which was to let Bobby Bewers off choir practice to run the Tillingfold scoreboard on Thursday evenings, and had taken the ten small boys, two women and three men and turned them into something very special. The Tillingfold Festival of Carols had already been shown on TV South. The other part of the bargain, undertaken willingly, was that the vicar did not sing himself. After cricket and a certain Spanish opera star, Tillingfold choir was Albert Jess's abiding passion.

Although Jess was more than twenty years older than his opening partner, the pair of them bore a strong resemblance to each other. Both were thin and wiry, loose-limbed natural athletes. Gauvinier wondered again as he watched them walk to the wicket if they were perhaps related in some way, although there was no mystery about either of their antecedents. Perhaps the centuries of inter-breeding among the Sussex villagers had produced the athlete as a type, just as another different recognisable Sussex feature was the tow hair and stocky build inherited from the sheep farmers of the days of William the Conqueror.

'Would you like first knock?' Jess, the regular opener made the offer. He knew that there is something quite out of the ordinary about opening the batting, no matter at what level of the game. Some people, like, say, Geoffrey Boycott of Yorkshire, would bat both ends and all day if possible. Others preferred to 'get the feel of things' by viewing proceedings from the bowler's end. Paul White had no such inhibitions. 'Anything you say, squire,' he replied, swishing at the longer pieces of grass with his bat. Jess glanced at him. He seemed genuinely unconcerned.

Okay. I'll face, then.' He felt bound to add: 'I usually do,' and felt absurdly put out when the boy commented: 'Ah, but you've usually got *James* at the other end,' with the accent heavily on the 'James'.

Jess grinned to show no offence taken, if any had been intended, and walked to the end of the wicket where the Wym keeper had already taken root.

'Right arm over', said the umpire, as Brown paced out his run. It was shorter than Norman Smith's, Jess saw, and at an angle of almost forty-five degrees to the list of the pitch itself. From the positions of his field setting, it seemed pretty certain that Brown was a devotee of an illustrious Gloucestershire predecessor. W.G. Grace, the great doctor, Jess had read, used to revel in the 'off-trap', and here was Brown with seven fieldsmen on the off side and only two on the leg. He counted them again to make sure. One, two, three slips; an old-fashioned point square and close to the wicket (almost 'silly' point, he thought); Cover point, a shortish mid-off, a long-off on the boundary and a deep extra cover. On the leg side there was just a man behind square leg and short mid-wicket.

'Good,' thought Jess, and pulled the first ball high and fairly wide past the bowler's right arm, safely into the empty deep field on the leg side.

'Come on. Two runs,' he called and scampered up the wicket. There was no fielder within thirty yards of where the ball pitched and indeed Jess thought it would run through for an unopposed four runs. As he turned for his second run he saw out of the corner of his eye the man running from the mid-off boundary.

'Only two,' he called. But White had slipped slightly on turning and he was only half way up the pitch when he saw the fielder gather the ball and hurl it towards the wicket. He still thought he could beat the throw-in to the bowler, who had turned to take it, but to his astonishment the ball hit the wicket when he was still a good yard out of his crease. Jess, alarmed by the sudden exultant appeal, could hardly believe his eyes as he turned to see White trailing a disconsolate bat on his way back to the pavilion.

'Strewth. That was one hell of a throw,' someone said. And the fielders all trooped over to congratulate Bruce, the fieldsman, who, cheerfully for him, admitted it was the first time he'd hit anything he'd aimed at since he'd been fighting Hitler's army. The silence in the Tillingfold ranks in the pavilion did nothing to console White, who threw down his bat with an excess of energy to a chorus of 'Bad luck, Paul.'

'Nobody's fault,' said Gauvinier, without much hope of pacifying him. And although White knew in his heart that that was true, and indeed had he shown as much urgency on the run as had the fieldsman in his throw, he might still have been at the crease. He still managed to blame Jess for the run-out. Just as Jess was doing, as the Wym scorer called out, 'Nought, one nought,' and was firmly checked by Budgeon: '*One*, one, nought.' 'Oh yes,' said the Wym man, 'I forgot about the first run.'

Jess met Gauvinier on the way to the wicket.

'I'm sorry Guv. I could have sworn there were two runs there.'

'So did everyone else,' said Gauvinier cheerfully. 'Let's get on with it.'

And little Jess put his head down and whacked Brown for two fours through his packed off-side field before the end of the over to put Tillingfold in better heart after such a disastrous start.

That Tillingfold got as near to their target as they did – they were eventually all out in the last over of the day for a hundred and ninety-two – was due in large measure to a sterling half-century by Jess, who felt he had something to atone for, to a tough stand of forty-three between Frank'n'Fred and a perfect piece of classical cricket from the Reverend Richard Veysey. He said afterwards that the trees put him in mind of Fenners, or the Parks (he had attended both Oxford and Cambridge) and he had scored thirty-five without giving a chance when Wym's schoolboy leg-spinner produced a googly that broke back through the gate and clipped his off-bail. Mr Veysey departed, conscious that the memory of two late cuts and a leg glance would sustain him as long as, if not longer than, the polished Graeco-Roman allusions in his text from the pulpit next Sunday. Both sides clapped his large and stooping figure from the field.

Gauvinier himself, did not stay long. He scored fifteen but underwent one of those days batsmen know when, for no reason he could find, he had no natural touch at all. The Wym bowling was if anything weaker than Tillingfold's. Brown was their best by far, and he was a trundler, as Jess said later. But no-one really collared his bowling, perhaps thanks to that inhibiting offside field. Gauvinier, having hit one four through the slips and one over the wicketkeeper's head, both unintentional, played what he considered to be a correct defensive forward stroke against Brown, only to see the ball travel gracefully in a low full-pitch to the lone mid-wicket, who went down on both knees to take the catch. It was not half as hard as he made it look, but as he explained afterwards: 'That's the first one I've held in three games.' Which excused the care, if not the attitude of prayer.

Trine made a few runs before being bowled, as usual, head up and aiming somewhere between Wym House and the setting sun, but Jess went on, batting with more and more confidence, so that it was a great shock when he was well caught behind the wicket slashing at a ball well out of his reach. He was both pleased with himself and mortified.

'Sorry, Guv. Should have had a ton today.' He wiped his sweating face. 'Oh yes, sorry Paul, too. I really thought . . .'

'Yeah,' said White, who'd had time to get over his disappointment at being out without facing a ball. 'I should have got in, Albert. I slipped a bit. Still, it was a bloody good throw.' As indeed it had been. He would remember the ball breaking the wicket in front of his outstretched bat for a long time.

By now it was half past six, four wickets were down and a hundred and ten on the board. If Tillingfold were going to win the match, it was up to the veterans of the side: Frank'n'Fred. Both, like Gauvinier, 'circling fifty', they had been doing this sort of thing for Tillingfold since they were boys. Frank Hunter, broad-shouldered, once trim in the hips but gone to seed, took his stance from his father – feet together, facing front almost as though playing 'French cricket'. It seemed impossible from such a stance that he could hit anything at all, but when he did so it was an astonishingly free movement on either side of the wicket. Trine's father, who fancied himself as a poor man's 'Spy', had drawn a cartoon of Tom Hunter in coloured crayon, which hung on the Tillingfold pavilion wall, and Trine's sister, who had inherited her father's talent, had drawn a similar one, at Trine's instigation, of Frank, to hang beside it. The two drawings looked like Tweedledum and Tweedledee from 'Through the Looking Glass'. Fred Bason, just as broad-shouldered but built 'like a brick shit-house' as he was wont to describe himself, for he was a builder, and a most successful one at that, held his cricket bat as though it were a shovel. Indeed, that is how it appeared to many opposing bowlers. The longer Fred stayed at the crease, the broader his blade appeared to become, and he scooped and shovelled any amount of unlikely runs.

These two, sweating, puffing and panting, shovelled and slashed, slashed and shovelled, and when both were out Tillingfold had a real chance to win, needing forty-five runs in the last ten overs of the game. Richard Veysey was at the crease, and had already made three or four strokes of the purest pedigree that might have been recognised at Lord's in the days when Peter May was king. But Tillingfold had only three batsmen left – Gillian Grantham, Norman Smith and Joe Deacon. Twice Gauvinier glanced across at Gillian, sitting tensely forward in her deckchair, and swallowed the urge to switch her with the men. He knew that technically she was by far the better bat than either Norman or Joe. Norman, for all his and Gauvinier's efforts, was like many a good bowler, temperamentally unsuited to holding a cricket bat. So long as he hit straight down the line, he might connect and make a useful run or two. Joe Deacon, on the other hand, had been a competent batsman until he had broken his elbow when his milk-float overturned and lost his nerve in the same accident. Curiously, it had not affected his wicketkeeping, which was as sharp as ever, but Gauvinier knew that Joe would step smartly to leg, away from his wicket, the moment any ball, no matter how slow, pitched a fraction short. However, wouldn't a man, *any* man, be better in a crisis than a girl?

With an effort which he acknowledged to himself with heavy irony, Gauvinier kept his doubts to himself and wished Gillian luck. She marched to the wicket jauntily, her cheeks flushed and her back that bit straighter because of the irrepressible White's wolf-whistle. Brown, the Wym skipper, had forgotten Tillingfold were fielding a girl in the side, and certainly had not expected to see her before last man in at number eleven. It was actually the first time he'd seen a girl batting, he thought, apart from a few seconds once on the TV news. He did not intend to make it easy for her, and she seemed competent enough in the way she took guard, looked round the field and settled into her stance. Brown brought the two leg-side fielders into within three yards of the bat, waved in the closer ones on the offside and bowled a slow long-hop on the middle stump. Gillian, right leg across and back towards the stumps, hooked the ball cleanly and hard to the square leg boundary, turning her wrists correctly to keep the ball flat along the ground. Square leg hopped smartly out of the way as the ball whistled past his ankle.

'No need to run for that. Well hit,' called the vicar, as the boundary was signalled. He walked down the wicket to her. 'Watch him. He's got a nasty gleam in his eye,' he warned her. And Brown delivered a fast, hard flat yorker right into the blockhole, which Gillian watched right onto the bat, and stopping it dead, the impact stinging her hands and wrists quite severely.

Brown eyed her. Chivalry, he thought grimly, does not belong on a cricket field. And he bowled her the meanest ball he knew, a fast, short inswinger, which would have been a 'bouncer' had he been fifteen years younger. The ball rose nastily, but once more Gillian's footwork had placed her correctly to deal with it. The ball dropped from the dead bat in front of her chest in the best approved defensive manner. Brown paused at the end of his follow through to look at her with respect. 'The lass can handle a bat,' he said to Veysey, who was watching the performance with his usual benign approval.

'Didn't you expect her to?'

'Not as well as that,' said Brown, frankly.

'Oh, Miss Grantham knows what she's doing,' said the vicar with some satisfaction. But his actions did not quite match his confidence, for he proceeded blatantly to 'farm' the bowling as much as he could. For a time all went well, and the animated watchers in the pavilion were able to believe – almost – that the match could and would be won. But Veysey's efforts came to an end with two overs still to go and twelve runs needed to win. He attempted another late cut off the ubiquitous Brown and, finding the ball much closer to his body than he expected, edged it gently into the wicketkeeper's hands.

Gauvinier refused to give up hope. Gill Grantham might get a couple of fours, one of Norman's swishes might connect. But Gillian managed two nice drives for two in the penultimate over and was forced to let Norman face the last one. Six balls to go; eight runs to win. Norman heaved mightily at the first ball, connected with air and heard the wickets go down behind him. Five balls to go. Eight runs to win. One wicket left. It was tense enough, and Joe Deacon backed away from his first ball, which struck an inside edge, missed the wicket by a fraction, evaded the wicketkeeper, and was only just stopped by a madly scrambling fine-leg on the boundary as the batsmen ran two precious runs. A sort of madness glazed Deacon's eye and he hit out at the next ball without backing away from it. Another inside edge brought him another two runs and another howl of exasperation from the keeper. Four runs to win now, but only three balls left. Could they do it? Deacon, reverting to type, backed away from the fourth ball of the over and watched with dismay as his last minute jab missed and the ball hit the off stump with a decisive 'click'.

Much as he would have liked to win, Gauvinier was not dissatisfied with the way his team had played. Beaten but not disgraced was a reasonable verdict, he felt, as he stood up to lead the applause for the Wym side, who in their turn gave Gillian a hand as she entered the pavilion with fourteen not out against her name in the scorebook. The two captains exchanged the time-honoured pleasantries, none the less sincere even though they came by rote.

'Congratulations, skipper. A most enjoyable game.'

'Oh, you fellows gave us a fright towards the end, there. If the luck had gone the other way, you'd have beaten us.'

'Well, I thought we might just sneak home. But it wasn't to be. You bowled well.'

'Thanks. I have to. Wym doesn't grow bowlers on

trees. See you in the pub.'

'Right.'

The arrangements were simple. There were no shower facilities in the little Wym pavilion ('And no bar, either,' as Trine said to Jess) but they were due to book in at the Shepherd's Crook for the night; so without changing they crammed their belongings and the cricket gear onto the Hunter Travel coach and Frank drove them slowly through the village. In the westering sun the Cotswold stone houses seemed picked out in honey, their tall eaves and diamond-leaded windows speaking of centuries of subservient prosperity. For more than a thousand years the Earls of Wym had owned and ruled this part of Wessex, and although death duties, capital transfer tax, capital gains tax and the like had caused the family to trim its sails a little, they had yet to make a significant inroad into a way of life which included sheep farms in Australia and the Argentine, a yacht at Cannes and a sugar plantation or two in the West Indies.

The big breweries of the West Country had long had their eye on the Shepherd's Crook, the only inn in the village and the centre of many square miles of fertile countryside, but the living, like that of Wym's Church of St John, the Wym Village Stores, the Wym Flower Mill (*sic*. Three centuries ago a signwriter whose artistic ability was not matched by his literacy had initiated a tradition) lay firmly in the gift of the Earl of Wym. And although he sat on the boards of at least two of the said brewers, the Shepherd's Crook remained a 'free house', boasting among its regular ales such esoteric brews as Newcastle Brown Ale and Singapore Tiger. The current holder of the licence, an unlikely Cockney known to all as 'Dave', although his name was Syd Blake, had been installed for three years, had doubled the turnover in that time and trebled the profits. His 'West Country Cabin' was making a name for itself as a restaurant where one could rely on superb English cooking (the chef was a smiling Vietnamese refugee) and Dave had badgered the Earl into letting him build the six double chalets (in stone, of course, and in harmony with the village architecture) in which the Tillingfold team were to spend the night.

'We didn't quite know what to do,' Brown told Gauvinier. 'We didn't know how much you chaps could afford, and so on, so we thought you'd make your own arrangements with Dave for this evening. They do a full three-course meal with wine thrown in for £12.50 a head, but we reckoned that would be too pricey for a tour, so Dave reckoned he could fit you up with chops or ham and chips for a couple of quid a time, if that suits. Just tell him how many and he'll see to it. Some of us'll be down to join you and Dave's got his licence extended. Should be a good night.'

It had, indeed, been a good night, Gauvinier reflected as at four o'clock the next morning he sat wearily on his bed and slid the shoes off his aching feet. A good night. Brown, Lord Wym and half a dozen of the home cricketers had joined the party in the Crook's dining room, where 'ham and chips' included a couple of fried eggs, salad and apple pie; where the Earl's offer of 'drinks on me' did not run out until well after normal closing time; where the 'late licence' apparently still had time to run when Gauvinier left at a quarter to four; and where Albert Jess had proved himself as expert (and nearly as loud) on the honky-tonk piano as ever he had been with an electric guitar and a hundred thousand dollars' worth of amplifier behind him.

It had started quietly, with the two teams mulling over the events of the day's play and gradually getting to know each other. Gillian was pleased that Brown and a couple of other Wym players had brought their wives with them – she did not want to be outnumbered twenty to one in a stag party, and there were a couple of unattached girls too. One was Lord Wym's daughter, Quincey, who showed every sign of being a very generous hostess indeed, especially where Edward Trine was concerned.

Gauvinier shared his thoughts with Brown and the Earl of Wym.

'It never fails to amaze me,' he said, 'how cricket seems to have something for everyone. Even James there' – he indicated Mitterman, soberly tucking into his ham and chips down the table – 'even James, who's no great shakes, helped get you out. Paul, our best batsman, was out without facing a ball, and yet he took a blinding catch. And had a run-out. Even Budgeon in the scorebox said he enjoyed the game.'

'He's the cripple, isn't he?' asked Lord Wym. 'Used he to play?'

'Not only did, he still does. He's been a regular member of our side for years. He was born with polio, you know, and it left him permanently deformed. He's our local cobbler, but cricket's always been the big thing in his life. He makes boots too – cricket boots. James, the treasurer, helps him with the business side. And Trine buys a pair every year, just to keep him going.'

He was interrupted by a call from down the table.

'Come on Guv. Who's the fines skipper today?'

'Fines? Oh, it's you, Bill. You've been doing nothing but fiddle the scorebook all day. Albert, you do the collecting.'

Jess drained his tankard as Budgeon hoisted himself awkwardly to his feet.

'Right now,' he said. 'Teddy first for dropping a sitter – 10p. And the skipper 10p for giving the bloke another go. And Teddy 20p for catching him second time round. Young Norm gets a 10p fine for dropping his catch, and only 5p for his overthrows, 'cause he's got to pay for a jug for six wickets and a hat-trick. There's another jug for Albert's fifty, 'n' 20p each for Frank'n'Fred for sharing a fifty partnership – they're too mean to get one for themselves. Gillian – 10p for hitting the opposing skipper for four, first ball – that's not polite, that isn't – and James for getting injured in the cause of duty.'

He paused to wait as Jess passed his tankard round for the coins to come jingling in.

'Now here's one I'm going to enjoy. There's a 50p fine for our umpire . . . for giving a man out after he's been hit in the face. Can't be right.'

Fanshawe joined in the general laughter. 'I'll cough up,' he said, 'but only if you'll tell us what you put in the score book, Bill.'

'Well,' said Budgeon. 'We didn't rightly know what to put. So I wrote 'caught' and my mate wrote 'hit wicket', and neither of us knew which was right. So I'd better fine myself as well.' And he dropped a coin into the tankard and sat down among applause. And stood up again.

'Oh yes, and there's another 10p for Albert for running out Paul. And 10p for Paul's blob. Another 10p for Norm's duck too. And 10p for Paul's four he let through his legs. And 10p for Frank getting us here without running out of petrol. And 20p for Joe for swearing under his breath – at least twice.'

He sat down again, with finality this time, and Mitterman accepted the coins with due gravity. 'Two pounds fifty,' he announced.

'What d'you do with the fines money?' asked Brown.

'We put it towards a bat for the most promising young player of the season,' Gauvinier answered. 'We used to throw a team party, but this way seemed more useful.'

'Ours is going towards a new pitch,' said Brown. 'Lord Wym here's pretty generous, but he can't do everything. We get the ground fee in perpetuity so long as we keep it up, and as you saw today that's now going to include a complete new square. Even if we cut all the corners that's £2,000 just for the marl and the turf, and we'll have to do all the laying ourselves.'

'How many members d'you have?' Gauvinier was curious.

'Just under fifty altogether, about twenty-five playing members. But we do a lot in the village. We hold an annual sports day to go along with the fête at the big house; we hold the village Christmas party and a Spring dance. We even run a mixed hockey side in the winter – though as you can see the field's not really up to it, and it can be a bit dangerous.'

Gauvinier grinned. His memories of mixed hockey were nothing if not bloodthirsty. This little gem-like village had, it seemed, much in common with the sprawling jumble of mingled ancient and modern that was Tillingfold.

'You seem to be pretty active,' he said.

'Yes,' said Brown. It's a funny thing. Just after the war the club nearly died, but a few of the old boys kept it ticking over until the Earl here came back and got things going again. Then the football club seemed to be all the rage, but that's been defunct for five years now, and the youngsters are coming back to cricket. There's great competition to get into our Colts side. They were county runners-up last year,' he added with pride.

That was virtually the end of any serious conversation, for a number of the younger players persuaded Jess to lift the lid of the old upright piano, and the real business of the evening commenced. A couple of his chart-topping numbers of ten years before went down well, but it wasn't long before he found himself vamping to the tunes his father had taught him. They all seemed to know the words – and the tunes – to 'Tipperary', 'There's a Long, Long Trail' and 'Silver Threads'; while Dave the landlord came out in his apron and absurd pork-pie hat and made them join in a whole series of cockney barrow-boy songs, bringing the house down with 'I'm Getting Married in the Mornin'', a tune that Gauvinier's now comfortably befuddled brain insisted on confusing with 'Lupino Lane'.

There were moments, of course. One was when Paul White threatened to black the other eye of Clive Archibald, who he considered was paying too close attention to Gillian, over whom he had assumed a quite unwanted proprietorial air. Gillian, feeling as though she were lumbered with two rather large and recalcitrant dogs, calmed them down by swearing undying devotion to all things Tillingfold, if not to Paul himself, and escaped to the chair next to

Gauvinier vacated by the Earl, who had gone to inspect his establishment's plumbing.

'Enjoying yourself?' he asked her quizzically.

She took the question seriously.

'You know, I am,' she said. 'There's always a bit of this heavy-breathing stuff, but when it gets a bit much I can always come and talk to you or to Mr Fanshawe about cricket. But I've had an idea. I'd like to write this tour up. For the club, with all the figures and so on. And a record of all the daft things people get up to on tour. It'd be rather fun. Although some people might not like to be reminded of everything that happened.' She looked down the room to where young Trine appeared to be inspecting the inside of the Hon Quincey Wym's rather flimsy blouse.

Another moment was when Paul White tried to drink a pint of strong Wessex ale standing on his head, and had to be led outside to be ill; and yet another came when Quincey Wym did a tap-dance on a table.

'Sorry, young man,' the Earl told Trine. 'I'm taking her home now. She'll be out like a light by the time I get her there and she'll be no use to man or beast for the next twenty-four hours. You can carry her to the car if you like.'

'Oh I say,' protested Trine. But Earl Wym knew his daughter, who took a small bow after her tap-dance and collapsed into Trine's arms. Making the best of a bad job, he hoisted her fireman's-style onto his shoulders and carried her from the room to a chorus of applause.

Jess struck up the conga on the piano. Gillian seized Gauvinier's hand and dragged him to his feet, grabbing him round the waist and forcing him into the kicking, swaying rhythm of the step. Round the chairs and tables went the human snake, out of the door, round the long-closed bars and back again. 'Da-da-da-da-da-con-*ga*. Da-da-da-da-da-con*ga*.' It was quite mad, quite foolish, and fun. Gauvinier sank into his chair, panting and laughing.

'Good god, I haven't done anything like that for years,' he said out loud. Gillian kissed him lightly on the cheek. She was hardly out of breath, but her eyes were dancing. 'You wait,' she said enigmatically. 'The tour's not over yet.'

He was still puzzling over what she might mean when he fell asleep.

In the morning he picked over a cautious piece of dried toast to go with his orange juice and black coffee and congratulated Dave, the landlord, on the immaculate state of his dining room. Dave seemed to be none the worse for having apparently been up all night. The only sign of the evening's revelry was a pile of tablecloths in one corner. All the tables were freshly laid in crisp white linen.

'Won't you get into trouble about your licence?' he asked the landlord as he brought him a fresh pot of steaming coffee. 'I mean, don't the police take an interest in what goes on?' He knew well what would happen in Tillingfold if the Dog and Duck were to serve quantities of liquor at four in the morning, late licence or no.

Dave looked at Gauvinier and decided he could be trusted.

'Oh, they do take an interest, sir. A close interest.' He moved across to the heap of tablecloths and lifted one corner of it. Underneath, flat on his back and dead to the world, was the corpulent figure of the Wym wicketkeeper. 'Meet Police Constable

Dockeridge,' said the landlord gravely, replacing the tablecloths gently.

Mitterman joined Gauvinier at the table and shook the skipper slightly by ordering a full breakfast of eggs, bacon and mushrooms; and one by one the Tillingfold team struggled in, each bearing the signs of the previous evening's festivities; all but Trine, who failed to put in an appearance until five minutes before the coach was due to depart, when he turned up panting slightly (having run the mile and a half from Wym House) but otherwise as fresh as a daisy, and ordered a double go at the bacon and eggs.

Jess, who knew full well where he had been, raised a chuckle.

'Teddy, I can't say I admire your taste, but I'm full of envy at your appetite,' he said. To which Trine merely replied: 'Makes you hungry, living in the country.' And he tucked into his second egg.

'Morning, Guv. I've got a bit of a problem, I think.' Norman Smith pulled up a chair and held out his right hand for Gauvinier's inspection. The upper two joints of the forefinger were swollen and contused, purple in colour and obviously exceedingly painful to the touch.

'Was it that catch?' he asked. It was always amazing how a dropped catch left its image behind, whereas if you clung on to a stinger you forgot the pain in a couple of minutes.

'That started it,' said Smith. 'Then there was the run-out. Then I caught it in the jamb of the door during the conga.'

'Well, you certainly won't be able to play today. Can you move it at all?'

Norman tried to waggle his finger. The finger moved slightly, and Norman said, 'Ouch!' The top joints seemed to be locked solid.

Gauvinier called Fanshawe over to inspect the injury.

'D'you think he'd better go for an X-ray?'

'What d'you think, Norm? Is it throbbing?'

Norman had a horror of hospitals.

'It'll be okay.' he said 'It's only stiff.' And indeed he like most cricketers had known the effects of a dislocated finger joint on more than one occasion. The fourth finger of Gauvinier's left hand was permanently twisted after he had broken it for the third time. Wicketkeepers especially, in spite of (or because of, Deacon would say) their protective gloves with rubber casings for the fingers, are particularly prone to arthritic finger joints from the constant battering. Even the best of them.

Paul White sauntered over, a large slice of marmalade and toast in his mouth, to add his expert opinion. 'That won't do your social prospects a lot of good, Norm,' he grinned. 'What did she do? Cross her legs?'

Norman flushed, for indeed he felt guilty in having enjoyed, even innocently, the company of one of the Wym girls during the evening. Jess came to his rescue.

'Don't listen to him. He's only jealous. And your name isn't Trine. Come on. Let's see what we can do for that finger.' And he led Norman off to the washroom, where he filled a glass with cold water and the basin with scalding hot, and made Norman spend five minutes plunging his unfortunate finger from one into the other, confident that this age-old remedy would have its effect. At the end of the treatment, even though it looked even more tender, Norman was able to make distinct movements of the joints and the prognosis had improved.

'At least you won't die yet.'

At least, thought Gauvinier, that's solved one of my little problems: both yesterday's non-players, Budgeon and Bobby Bewers, must be given a game today. And although Norman Smith, as his only bowler with any pace, would have been the last player he would normally have left out, circumstances were forcing his hand.

The Reverend Richard Veysey solved the second problem.

'I'm afraid I'll have to drop out, too, Peter. Touch of the old trouble.'

The Veysey 'old trouble' was not, as might be imagined, an aching back, but what might be described as an occupational hazard for a priest: namely housemaid's knee. In his youth, briefly but vividly recalled during hs innings against Wym, Richard Veysey had been a very fine athlete indeed, deprived of a double-Blue only by severe injuries to the cartileges of both knees, which corrective surgery had failed to alleviate, and which had meant that pursuit of his chosen profession was a daily pilgrimage of pain. Every time Richard Veysey knelt to pray his knees gave him hell. Gauvinier was one of the few people who knew what it cost him every time he called 'Let us pray.'

'Okay, Richard. Perhaps you'll fight it out with Norman who'll keep the scorebook. Just as long as Bobby here isn't ashamed of it.'

Bobby, whose expertise with the Tillingfold scorebook had brought him a reputation in Sussex second only to that of the great Bill Frindall of BBC fame, grinned. In fact he was only too happy to have left the scorebook behind him, and yesterday had persuaded Budgeon to carry out the chore, leaving him free to 'chat up' the Wym girls. Old Bill would always help a fellow out; and Bobby had made any amount of small errands and deliveries for Bill while he was still a choirboy. Now approaching sixteen, he was more than anything eager to make himself a permanent niche in the Tillingfold team. Although his talent would never outrun his enthusiasm for the game, Gauvinier had in fact marked him down as a future Tillingfold captain.

'He's the salt of the earth, that kid,' he had told Fanshawe over many a pint in the Dog and Duck. 'He's only got two ambitions: to play for England, and Tillingfold. Nothing else. To hell with the county or the Martlets or the big clubs. Just Tillingfold. Or England. Can you explain it?'

Fanshawe couldn't, any more than he could explain why Gauvinier, who might have had the ability, or Jess, or even Mitterman, who could have bought his way into any club in the land had he so desired to do so, stuck it out with a village side like Tillingfold. He wanted to suggest that it had something to do with Gauvinier himself, but knew that Gauvinier would ridicule such nonsense, just as he knew that if Gauvinier were suddenly to depart, for whatever reason, then another skipper would take over and the club would move along into another generation, hiccuping perhaps, but still moving. Nor could Fanshawe explain why this should be so, nor the fascination which this peculiarly English game should hold over these grown and active men. Even he, middle-aged wreck that he was, found the very means to keep going in the sport in which he could only play a peripheral (even if vitally important) part as an umpire. So he always answered Gauvinier's rhetorical question in the same way. 'Oh, you're all bloody fools, you cricketers.'

And Gauvinier would counter, with the utmost affection: 'Ah, look who's talking.' And life would be just a little warmer.

Chapter Five

THE TILLINGFOLD CRICKET CLUB had made it a tradition over the years to bring on young players; and Bobby Bewers, ex-choirboy turned budding cricketer, was the latest beneficiary of the policy. He had been the first to win the yearly award of a cricket bat paid for by the modern 'fines' system, which had taken over perfectly adequately the burden the Club President, Sir Edgar Trine, DSO etc., had carried out with decreasing generosity for the past thirty years. Gauvinier had inherited as captain the task of maintaining the club's kit bag, another amenity which some members felt should be abolished, but which Gauvinier felt passionately was essential.

'But, Peter,' James Mitterman (and others) would argue. 'In this day and age everyone who calls himself a cricketer has a bat, pad and gloves, at least. Anyone can afford these things these days. They shouldn't be playing cricket if they can't afford them.'

But Gauvinier argued stoutly for the value of the club bag. He knew that although even a natural layabout like Paul White could sport his own bat (and a very good one at that) it was a different matter when it came to the rest of the kit. These days, he reckoned, counting up the items, it would take a good £300 to kit a youngster out to play, even for Tillingfold, were it not for the club bag. A decent bat – by that he meant a reputable English bat made of English willow with a decently sprung handle – would cost a minimum of £45. The cheapest of boots would take another £25; though if you went to a specialist like Budgeon, he would make you a pair for £120. Pads: say £15. Batting gloves: £12. A plastic box would do (no-one bothered what you pushed down the front of your trousers): a couple of quid. A decent pair of slacks would set you back £25 or more; shirts, even at Marks and Spencer, £20; while you could pay anything up to £10 for a pair of socks and twelve times that for a real woollen sweater, authentically cable-stitched. If you were a bowler, you could count on running through at least three pairs of boots a season, even playing for a village side like Tillingfold; two pairs of flannels a season, perhaps three if it was a wet one. Two bats – three if you made more than a few runs. Even if you took it easy, a season's cricket would cost a couple of hundred quid; and then there was the club subscription, the match and tea fees which seemed to rise inexorably every year, and the inevitable costs at the bar or in the pub afterwards.

'It's getting as bad as the nineteenth hole,' was a common complaint at the clubs, as more and more enlarged their premises, and more and more brewers came forward obligingly with the capital to put in a bar, cheerfully undercutting the livelihoods of their own pub landlords, often just the other side of the village green.

As soon as he could wangle himself out of the scorebox, which was as soon as his voice had broken and as soon as he could begin to wield a 'Harrow' size bat with a degree of competence, young Bewers had taken over the unofficial title of baggage-master to the Tillingfold side. No longer did odd pads from other clubs find their way into the Tillingfold dressing room. No longer was a right-handed batsman sent to the wicket wearing two left-handed gloves (or two right-handed ones for that matter). No longer were they a bat short on away matches; the bails always matched and the umpire's coats came out white each week as though they had been freshly laundered – as indeed they had. When some longer hitter than usual, like Paul White, had deposited a ball in the depths of the adjacent thicket, not to be found until the following spring, young Bobby would come forward on the instant with a replacement; and should the visiting club fail to have brought a new ball with them for the match, then Bobby (at the drop of a £20 note) would produce a plum-red sphere shining with newness and marked 'Made in England'. Not Pakistan, or India, or Australia, or anywhere else. Made in England.

On a tour like this, one such as Bobby was invaluable, as hardly needs to be spelt out. And if there were some mutterings among the older playing members that 'the youngsters are always favoured,' Gauvinier could retort that if they, the older members, put in half the work for the club as did some of the young'uns, then there'd be no worry at all for the future. He was so glad to have Bobby and his cheerful helpfulness along that he had not even asked how the boy had been able to afford the £40 they had to charge everyone on tour, for the basic cost of the fuel and accommodation. Frank Hunter had let the club have the coach free of charge, of course, and was driving it himself to save the cost of a driver, but there was still diesel fuel and the hotel charges to be met. Everyone paid for their own drinks, of course, apart from the kitties, and the older, better-off players usually saw to it that the younger ones didn't go short.

On the way to the West Country from Tillingfold the previous day, the travellers had sustained themselves with several bursts of singing interspersed with much good-humoured banter. But today's shorter trip was more subdued, particularly as Trine, usually the leader in such things, plumped himself down in his seat and promptly fell fast asleep. Bobby enlisted the aid of Budgeon and Gillian, and spread the contents of the club bag along the back seat, carefully touching up the pads with white Padawax and discreetly rubbing down the worst of the marks on the bats with fine sandpaper. For an hour or so the coach eased its way lazily through half a dozen villages identical to Wym, rising and dipping through the rolling hills. Then through a maze of twisting lanes and hamlets, each a little bigger than a series of farm buildings, and out into broader country with strangely nondescript scenery. At one o'clock they found the motel where they were to spend the second night. They piled out stiffly.

'Bit of a come-down, this, after Wym.' Jess's thought was shared by almost everyone as they surveyed the drab square cabins. But in fact the rooms were comfortable and surprisingly cool on such a hot day; the salad in the square dining room with its plastic curtains was fresh, and the ham ('What, again?') honey-cured and sweet; and in good heart they rolled onto the green Brocester recreation ground, to be greeted by a large man with a square face to match his shoulders. His tweed trousers were held up by braces and his sleeves were rolled up, revealing forearms like hams.

He shook each member of the team enthusiastically by the hand as they emerged from the coach. His vowels were as broad as his shoulders.

'I'm Sam. Sam Thatcher. No relation, unfortunately. Never had a bloody grocer in the West Country Thatchers. Or a politician for that matter. I'm a farmer. And the club secretary. Glad you're on time. Have you had a good trip so far? We're looking forward to meeting you. The pitch is in pretty good shape. We had over a thousand people here on Sunday.'

He led the way across the trimly-mown outfield to the wide low pavilion which looked to Gauvinier as though it had been hijacked from an army surplus store, spraying out questions and snippets of information in an unending stream.

'Best little club in Somerset, this. We got to the quarter-finals of the Cup this year. Twenty coaches and over three hundred cars. Two thousand people. You comfortable at the motel? If you're not, just let me know. I'll fix the landlord. He's a member. What's wrong with your lad's hand? Finger? My wife will fix that. She's an SRN. Daughters do the tea. Pavilion? Yes. The old one burnt down and we bought the huts from an old RAF camp. Put them all up ourselves, built the bar and made a thousand pounds profit last year. We run the Somerset Beer Festival and the Scrumpy Season too. People come from all over. We put in that artificial pitch last year, so it doesn't matter if it rains. Not that it will today.' He looked up at the clear blue of the sky and laughed hugely.

Gauvinier thought that Mr Thatcher the farmer must be something of a politician, and a businessman too, if he was the driving force behind this go-ahead and apparently successful little club.

A small group of men in white flannels in varying states of repair stopped throwing a ball among themselves and came to meet the visitors. Sam introduced Gauvinier to his opposite number – a large fair man with a pear-shaped figure. He was wearing a wicket-keeper's glove on his left hand and he carried a bat in his right. He tucked the bat under his arm and enveloped Gauvinier's hand in a huge paw. 'Phil Shaw,' he said. 'Captain Shaw, like in Gilbert and Sullivan. Good to see you.' If anything his vowels were broader than Mr Thatcher's. 'I suppose he's told you the history of Brocester as you came across.'

'Just about.' Gauvinier laughed. Shaw's sturdy figure was already bent over a battered but capable-looking motor mower. 'He seems to do most things.'

Phil Shaw grinned. 'He does just about. What did he call himself to you? Secretary? Old Sam's chairman of the club too, did he tell you that? And he was captain until two years ago when he reached sixty and his doctor told him not to be such a bloody old fool. He still plays for the second team on Sundays. You couldn't keep him out. But he's done wonders for this club.'

Gauvinier watched the sturdy figure following the mower up and down the square.

'What about his farm? Shouldn't he be getting the harvest at this time of year?'

'Oh, he just says he pays other people to do that,' said Shaw. 'He does all this because he likes it. He was here all day yesterday putting a new boiler in the showers ready for you lot. Hope it works. What old Sam fixes usually does. After a fashion.' He indicated the door of the visitors' dressing room. 'In there lads.

No, sorry miss. That's the team room. Ladies' room's the other side, behind the bar.'

Gillian smiled at him.

'That's all right, captain. I'm in the team.'

The news seemed to dumbfound Mr Shaw. He turned to Gauvinier.

Gauvinier grinned. 'That's right, skipper. Miss Grantham is one of us.'

'Well, I dunno. We'll have to think about this. We've never played a woman before.' He placed such an emphasis on the 'woman' that Gauvinier understood this to be a genuine crisis. 'I'll have to go and talk to the lads.'

He marched into the home dressing room, shutting the door behind him. The Tillingfold team stood undecided, listening to the rise and fall of his voice through the door. Soon there came the sounds of disbelief, followed by a babel of questioning voices.

The door opened.

'Well, they don't like it, and that's a fact,' said Shaw. 'Nor more don't I. We ain't never played a woman before. What are we supposed to do. Bowl underarm?'

'Look,' said Gauvinier. 'It's a bit of a shock, I know. Let me talk to your team. It was a bit of a shock in Sussex too, when we started . . .'

The Brocester team crowded out of the dressing room, staring with frank curiosity at Gillian. She felt as though she was in a zoo. Gauvinier came straight to the point.

'This is Gillian Grantham,' he said. 'She's our number seven bat and right-arm change bowler. So far this year she's taken . . .' He turned to her. '. . . Sixteen wickets for a hundred and twenty-three runs. And she's scored . . . a hundred and fifty-nine runs.

That's right, isn't it Gill?'

'With a hard ball?' Someone at the back of the Brocester team laughed and flicked a cricket ball in Gillian's direction. She caught it one-handed, feinted and flicked it back underarm deceptively fast. The thrower grabbed at it, missed and doubled up as the ball thudded into his midriff.

'Miss Grantham doesn't need favours,' said Gauvinier, ushering his team into the dressing room, including Gillian. The Brocester team gathered none too sympathetically round their fallen hero.

'That'll teach you to be a smart-ass,' said Shaw. 'Women cricketers! We'll show 'em.'

It promised to be the sort of 'needle' that had been missing from the game at Wym, although when the two captains walked out together for the toss Shaw was at pains to reassure Gauvinier. It's nothing personal, you know,' he said. 'It's just that the lads never thought of playing cricket with a girl.' He put a wealth of meaning into the word. Gauvinier laughed.

'Oh Gillian's okay, as you'll see. You'll be surprised.' He changed the subject. 'My, this looks like a county class wicket.'

'Oh yes, it's pretty good. Old Sam sees to that. We've had several county Colts matches here.'

Gauvinier thought that Tillingfold might well pitch a wicket on the outfield. He said so. Shaw pointed across the field to the biggest roller he had ever seen; a giant horse mower with the original shafts still in position and slung between them a triangular contraption obviously used to connect onto a tractor tow-bar. 'When he's got nothing better to do, Old Sam sends for a tractor down from the farm and pulls the roller round a couple of times. Heads or tails?'

The two pairs of eyes followed the spinning coin into the sun.

'Heads,' called Gauvinier. 'Ah, that's a change. We'll bat, if you don't mind.' He prodded the firm turf to reassure himself, and Shaw laughed.

'Don't worry. There are usually plenty of runs in it for both sides.'

It was unusual for Gauvinier to choose to bat first. He held strongly to the theory that it was more attacking to put the other team in; he liked Tillingfold to have a target to aim at and he preferred to 'chase' rather than calculate the precise timing of a declaration, particularly when the strength of the opposition was unknown. But today's deciding factor was the damage to Norman Smith's finger. The absence of his main bowler (and only one of any speed) would seem on this pitch to constitute an invitation to Brocester to score at will. Not only was the pitch good, but the outfield looked lightning fast, with the grass browning under the hot sun, and very smooth.

'Get your pads on, Albert, please; and you too, James.' Gauvinier took the batting order he had prepared on the coach from his pocket and pinned it up on the dressing-room door. The players clustered round to read it.

1. Jess
2. Mitterman
3. White
4. Gauvinier
5. Bewers
6. Trine
7. Grantham

8. Hunter
9. Bason
10. Deacon
11. Budgeon

'Now take a look at the bowling first, but don't forget we want a lot of runs on the board before we see you again.' The Tillingfold attitude was always that the game was there to be got on with and the ball was there to hit; and of them all only Mitterman was genuinely incapable of opening his shoulders against the simplest of bowling. Strangely, after four overs bowled by Brocester, Mitterman had scored twelve runs to Jess's nine and, thanks to two leg byes that went for four, the score stood at twenty-nine for no wickets.

Both Mitterman and Jess found the Brocester opening bowler, a lanky individual well-named Long, but called 'Ploddy' by his team-mates, a real handful. He took a very long run and bowled fast left arm over the wicket with a loose-limbed action that even on this wicket made the ball fizz through, obliging the keeper (the captain, Shaw) to stand a good twenty yards back. Fortunately the bowler's length and direction were erratic, and Mitterman's tentative prods sent the ball flying off the edge of the bat, severely menacing the fingers and marital prospects of a formidable array of slipfielders.

His first four streaked between second and third slip and had to be fished gingerly out of the blackthorn hedge which lined the ground some fifteen yards outside the boundary. His second was the product of a stroke that is usually known as a Chinese cut, but is more correctly a drive aimed in the direction of mid-off which ends up as four runs over the fine-leg boundary, having narrowly evaded the wicket and the dive to leg by the wicketkeeper. And Mitterman's third and final boundary flew high off the shoulder of his bat, past his startled chin and just out of reach of Shaw's jump, pitching just short of the boundary and clattering into the white wooden sightscreen.

Mitterman was then only too relieved to receive Long's first straight ball, a beauty which yorked him, the ball seeming to pass clean through his tentative stroke and removing the middle stump clean out of the ground. Long performed an acrobatic cartwheel in imitation of the stump, and proceeded to beat the next batsman, White, all ends up with his next three balls without, however, getting so much as a touch of the bat or the wicket. He retired to the long-leg boundary to a deserved round of applause and the respect, not to say apprehension, of the Tillingfold batsmen.

Jess and White met in the middle of the pitch.

'Bastard's fast,' said White, patting down an imaginary bump with the toe of his bat.

'True,' said Jess. 'But he can be hit. Watch out for the odd good one. But I reckon if we can get him away once or twice he might crack up.'

'Who're you kidding? I didn't see one of those three balls.' Which was a slight exaggeration, as he had exceptionally quick eyesight and reactions, and had watched each of the three fly past and over his off stump without even trying to fend them off.

Jess grinned. He knew his man. 'Go on. You're just testing him.' And back he went to his own end of the wicket to face the less bombastic but more subtle skills of a balding bowler with a Zapata moustache and a strongly weather-beaten countenance. He had a way of shrugging his shoulders and head, and bringing his arm over high – 'Just like a cat washing its ears,' said Gillian, who was sitting watching with Gauvinier – to deliver the ball at a brisk medium pace. Jess had found him accurate, nagging away with good length inswingers and difficult to hit; and this over he produced a 'wobbler' which had Jess groping outside his off stump and missing, leading to a swift movement and appeal behind him. Jess looked at the square-leg umpire, who happened to be Fanshawe, and saw the finger go up. He had not heard the wicketkeeper tiptoe up into position behind him, and he looked back down at his toe, still poised on the popping crease.

'Damn,' he muttered softly to himself, knowing full well the wicketkeeper's axiom, 'The line is mine.'

'That was a bit swift.' He acknowledged the keeper's ability, confirmed by Gauvinier as they crossed. 'That was a damned fast piece of work, Albert. Bad luck.'

'Yes, you'd better watch him.' But in fact, although Shaw's speed with the gloves did inhibit the Tillingfold batsmen a little, he had no further successes throughout the innings. Once Gauvinier got his eye in, he forgot all about the keeper's menacing presence. Shaw had not been wrong about the pitch. It was a beauty, the ball coming through fast and true onto the bat and nothing unexpected about the bounce. In contrast to his hesitant form of the previous day, Gauvinier began to enjoy himself. He liked a duel with a fast bowler, and Long was good enough to make him work for his runs, but not so accurate as to tie him down. Gauvinier indulged himself with a leg glance fine to the boundary and then another wide to fine-leg's left hand, making the fielder run and stretch in vain for the speeding ball.

He had scored twenty-five and felt set for a big innings when Shaw took the moustachioed opener off and tossed the ball to an elderly man who had been fielding none too energetically at mid-on. He had a brown head as bald as a cricket ball and a brown beak of a nose, as if he had spent his whole life in the sun.

Gauvinier studied the faded cream flannels and thick shirt with sleeves rolled down even in the sunshine. The old brigade indeed. He wondered what type of bowling the oldster would produce. 'Left arm round the wicket,' called the Brocester umpire. Gauvinier felt rather than heard Shaw close up on the wicket behind him. The field was the orthodox slow left-arm bowler's setting – six men on the off side, three on the leg.

'Would you mind standing back, Mr Umpire, please?' The bowler took four strides from the left hand side of the wicket, crossed in front of the umpire and delivered the ball from a high upright stance. Gauvinier could see it spinning in the sunlight as it came through the air towards him, pitching on a length on his off stump and drawing him forward to play the ball carefully on the half-volley, left wrist cocked to tilt the bat forward, the ball spinning off the face of the bat towards the gully fielder. Three more similar balls followed, forcing Gauvinier into the utmost care. The fourth floated gently in with the bowler's arm and took the inside edge of Gauvinier's bat, causing the bowler suddenly to throw up his hands and check an involuntary appeal as the batsmen ran an easy single. Gavuinier felt a healthy respect for the bowler, and was somewhat mortified when White, a young man with no inhibitions, drove him cleanly through the covers off the last ball of the over.

Gavuinier had time to play his favourite shot off the

fast bowler, a late late cut delicately placed between first and second slip for four more runs, before unaccountably losing patience against the old left-arm bowler, stepping down the pitch to drive and hitting a skimming catch to deep extra cover. The fielder went down on one knee to take the ball, but never looked like dropping it, and Gauvinier was on his way to the pavilion mentally kicking his impulsiveness almost before the ball was fairly in the fielder's hands. His departure led to a mini-collapse, for Bobby Bewers quickly got a trimmer from Long which removed the off bail almost with the wind of its passing; and Trine hit the slow man for two thumping sixes before slicing a third attempt high into the air down to third man, where 'Ploddy' took a tumbling catch to the applause of his team-mates, ending on his back with his arms and legs in the air like a stranded crab, but with the ball clutched safely in one hand. At ninety-five for five Gauvinier could see Tillingfold's innings deteriorating quickly; but Paul White was still batting well, and was welcoming Gillian to the crease.

'Don't worry Gill,' he greeted her cheerfully. 'Stick around and let me do the work. I'll take the quickie for a bit, if you like.'

But Gillian was not to be patronised. 'I'll manage on my own, thank you,' she said with dignity. But White was batting too well to be put out. He patted her lightly on the bottom with his cricket bat, knowing it would rile her. 'Of course you will, Gill,' he said cheerfully. 'But watch that one. He's got designs on you.' He pointed to 'Ploddy', who was indeed thinking up a fearful vengeance for this young girl who dared to invade the man's preserve.

Unfortunately for Long, he was getting somewhat

tired after an hour and a quarter's bowling under hot sun, and in consequence was growing ever more erratic. In his determination to deliver a faster ball than ever he let the ball slip from his fingers, hurling a 'beamer' straight at Gillian's head. There was nothing she could do about it but get out of the way, which she did in the least dignified manner of all, sitting down abruptly on her backside and with some difficulty avoiding hitting the stumps with her bat. She glared angrily down the wicket.

'Steady on, Ploddy,' called Shaw, who had stopped the wild delivery with some difficulty himself. Muttering to himself, the bowler went back to his mark and, trying too hard to control the ball, sent down another full-length full-toss, but of a much more gentle pace, which Gillian met with the full face of the bat and dispatched over long leg's head for six. Determined as she was to show no emotion, she could not help a grin playing round her mouth as she shaped up to the next ball, driving it comfortably into the off field for two. 'Attagirl,' White said as they crossed for the second run.

Whether Brocester were demoralised by being hit around by a girl Gauvinier never found out, but the pair put on sixty runs in the next eight overs and when Gillian was finally bowled by a spinner Tillingfold had advanced to a hundred and seventy-three for six, with White sixty not out. Fifteen minutes later Gauvinier declared, reckoning that at a quarter to five he could try to give his bowlers time to bowl the home side out; and that Brocester too must be given a sight of the target if they were to go for the runs and not 'shut up shop'.

Tea was substantial and served in a marquee next

to the pavilion by a bevy of pretty girls consisting mainly, Gauvinier gathered, of Sam Thatcher's wife and daughters. Paul White, hero of the innings, came in for much welcome attention, but the main attraction for the Brocester players was Gillian. They couldn't get over her performance.

'Hitting Ploddy for six. Never seen anything like it.'

'Where d'you get them muscles, girl?'

'What did you score in the end, lass?'

'Oh, thirty-one, I think.'

'Bloody well done.'

'I told you she could handle herself well enough,' Gauvinier said quietly in Shaw's ear.

'Right enough, you did. I reckon old Ploddy learned a lesson or two.'

'Why "Ploddy"?'

'Mr Plod the policeman. He's Sergeant Long, and he plays for us because he says he gets a better game than with the police. But your young lady showed him who was boss.'

The young lady and the sergeant were in fact getting on very well indeed, Gauvinier saw with satisfaction. He had backed her into a corner and was earnestly questioning her about where she had learned her cricket.

'Oh, school, and Loughborough.'

'Why d'you play for Tillingfold? What's wrong with women's cricket?'

'It doesn't really interest me. And in any case, I'd have to go up to London to find a regular team, and I prefer to live in the country.'

'Don't you ever get hurt?' he asked, eyeing her softer parts speculatively.

'Not so far,' she said, blushing slightly. 'Some girls

wear chest-protectors. I don't. I try to keep out of the way of bouncers. And beamers.'

Sergeant Long had the grace to blush.

'I'm sorry about that,' he said seriously. 'It slipped.'

'So did I. I must have looked quite a sight, flat on my backside,' said Gillian.

'Ah but you got your own back, next ball. That was some shot, that six.'

'It's the first six I've ever hit,' she said.

'And it won't be the last,' said the sergeant gallantly.

But tea and chivalry had come to an end, and before he could make further progress he was called by his captain to 'turn his arm over' at the Brocester opening batsmen who had padded up and wanted to get their eyes in before going out to do battle.

The previous day Tillingfold had narrowly failed to reach a target of a hundred and ninety-nine; today they were defending a hundred and ninety-four, just five runs less. With Norman Smith fit and bowling at his best, Gauvinier would have been confident of subduing most village teams; without Smith, Tillingfold were going to have to struggle.

He threw the ball to Budgeon, who tossed it back at him.

'Which end d'you want, Bill? You've got a long evening ahead of you.'

'That's all right, Guv. It doesn't matter.' Budgeon's cheerful willingness was always a tonic. 'Who are you going to put on at the other end?'

'Ah.'

That was the problem. He must at least present Brocester with the semblance of an opening attack. Hunter and Bason were both too slow, particularly on such a fine wicket. Gillian at best was medium pace, as he was himself. And young Bewers was far too raw. He studied the Brocester opening batsmen. Both looked competent, seasoned cricketers. There was only one thing to do. He would have to lead from the front.

'I'll take the first over myself, Bill. From this end.'

Gauvinier had never liked opening the bowling. He knew his resemblance to Garfield Sobers stopped abruptly at the fact that they both bowled left-arm. Not for Gauvinier the fast-swinging opening spell, the orthodox follow-up and the rolling 'Chinamen' that the great West Indian could switch on at will to devastating effect. Gauvinier's pleasant left-arm pace at its best could sometimes break through a side with its accuracy and subtle changes of length and direction; but on a day like this with no cloud in the sky and a perfect batting strip, Gauvinier knew he would be lucky to take one wicket, let alone any more.

However, he lengthened his usual run to fifteen paces, gave himself the indulgence of two slip fielders (as much to keep the batsmen guessing as in the hope of taking a wicket there) and ran up to deliver his first ball, determined to concentrate on those two vital criteria, line and length. Somewhat to his surprise, he managed a maiden over, the batsman treating his deliveries with somewhat exaggerated respect. It did not escape Gauvinier's notice, however, that each ball was met firmly with the full face of the bat; there was never a hint of weakness in the steady defence.

Gauvinier had learned over the years to rely on Budgeon for all-out effort. He had known the cobbler since a child. Little Billy, as he'd been known forty years ago, had been born with polio, and the disease had left his legs permanently crippled, one shorter than the other and both bent outwards at the knees so that he walked in an ungainly shuffle, and to run at all he was forced into a clumsy stuttering canter, always dangerously close to disaster.

But Little Billy had grown up into Old Bill, his legs still uncrossed and his feet still encased in clubbed boots. He had apprenticed himself to his father and in due course, when the old man died, had taken over the little shop at the far end of the main street and continued to practise his trade as his father had before him. Among his contemporaries he had been a figure both of amusement and respect; 'Hopalong' they'd called him, after a famous cowboy hero of the time, but although the disability persisted, the name did not stick. There was something about young Billy's determination to pursue a normal life despite his handicap that impressed itself on the boys of the village. Billy joined in all their games, keeping goal at football, bowling and batting at cricket and fielding in the slips. They came to notice that anything within range of those massive hands was never dropped, no matter how hard, fast or unexpected it was. Billy held a cricket bat loosely, like a toy, and cracked the ball very hard, particularly to leg, but his bowling was his most remarkable accomplishment. Off a few shuffling paces his arm came over wide and so low it was almost round-arm; but there were very few boys in the village who could collar his bowling. Once in his groove, Bill Budgeon would deliver over after over of flat, medium-paced, good length balls, and on a pitch with any help at all he could be lethal. His best average was seven for fifteen against a local village early one May, when the Tillingfold pitch had almost the consistency of glue. He forced his way into the Tillingfold team when he was seventeen, and for thirty years had been one of its most stalwart members.

He bowled nineteen overs that August afternoon against Brocester, and took four wickets for eighty-eight. In the end he was so weary he could hardly force himself into his six-pace shuffle up to the wicket, but still found the strength and enthusiasm to catch Sergeant Long off a hard straight drive, low down and to his right, in his eighteenth over. He fell in a cloud of dust and grass seed, clutching the ball in his big brown hand, blinking the sweat out of his eyes and grinning at Gauvinier as he hauled him to his feet.

'Don't worry Guv, we'll do it.'

But Tillingfold didn't do it, not for all Budgeon's efforts, nor those of Gauvinier, Gillian, Bason, Hunter and Bewers, all of whom were tried at the other end. Gauvinier took one wicket – that of Shaw, his opposing skipper, who hit twenty-nine quick runs and then knocked his bails off swinging round in the hook. Gillian did better. She had two batsmen caught on the boundary by Trine and Jess, but the Brocester batsmen kept steadily piling on the runs and won comfortably enough by three wickets with a couple of overs to go.

'You can come again,' Shaw said half-joking as he shook hands all round after the game. 'And you too, miss.'

'I know,' said Gauvinier. 'You mustn't offend your hosts by winning. Thanks for the game.'

Shaw grinned. 'Never mind. We'll come up your way next summer and you can have your revenge. But don't produce a team of girls. They'd whack us out of sight.'

Gauvinier assured him that the lasses of Tillingfold had not come flocking in numbers to join Gillian to break down the ramparts of male privilege.

'Glad to hear it,' said Shaw. 'But what's intriguing

me at this moment is how you're going to sort out Old Sam's shower.'

On investigation, this turned out to be a problem indeed. Sam Thatcher's shower was designed to take two persons, and because of the limitations of space, these two would inevitably be in close, not to say intimate proximity. It was not what Gillian had in mind, whether with Tillingfold or Brocester, so she took the coward's way out and went to have a cup of tea with Mrs Thatcher and the girls as they finished the teatime washing up. In the end, it meant a cold shower when the men had finished, but it seemed the most sensible way out. By the time she joined them in the bar, the party was well under way.

Afterwards, the Tillingfold tourists reckoned it was the best night of the tour; but that was after some of the excesses of the evening had faded conveniently from their memories. It all started in the bar at the cricket club, when Trine and White challenged the prime of Gloucester's youth to a darts match. Soon this spread to a full-scale cricket match on the darts board, with each member of the team taking it in turn to 'bat'. Gillian, who knew little of darts and cared less, was carried shoulder high round the room by Trine and White when she threw a treble twenty and a bull to win the match for Tillingfold. The Tillingfold cheers nearly brought the roof down.

'Skittles. We'll take you on at skittles.' Phil Shaw joined in the Brocester cry and, led by Sergeant Long and the elderly spin bowler, the two teams erupted across the cricket field to the King William IV, an ancient and dignified public house which stood at the crossroads in the centre of the village.

'Skittles' turned out to be played, not in a long alley

like that of the Dog and Duck back home, but on an octagonal table, with the cue-ball at the end of a string tied to a pole at the side of the table. In the confined space of the public bar the innocent public was protected by a net slung from the ceiling round the table, but with two teams crowding round and the ninepins flying fast and furious, it seemed only a matter of time before someone was hurt. Gauvinier and Shaw prudently retired with Bason, Veysey and some of the older members of the teams to the relative peace of the 'private' bar or 'lounge', which was furnished with deep old leather settees and, as Gauvinier noticed with gratitude, no piped music. He mentioned this to Shaw.

'We got together in the village and told the brewers that if they put in a juke-box or anything like that we'd run them out of business,' said Shaw. 'They didn't like it, but the cricket club's doing so well they couldn't afford to get across us. We said they could have the music in the club for the youngsters; and over here we could enjoy our beer in peace.' He paused as a roar of applause and shouting broke out from the public bar. 'Well, relative peace, anyway.'

Fanshawe stirred. 'Tell me something about the club,' he said. 'You seem to be doing extraordinarily well for such a small place.' He looked across the darkening field to the cricket club. 'There doesn't appear to be much around here to support it.'

'It's deceptive,' Sam Thatcher said, lighting his pipe. 'There aren't many houses here but there are at least twenty hamlets within five miles of Brocester. There's been a cricket club here since the 1880s – no-one knows quite how long. So we're at least a hundred years old. The ground belongs to the District Council, but as it was given to them in perpetuity as a recreation field for the people of Brocester, they can't do anything with it. There were some councillors after the last war who wanted to build houses on it, but the cricket club – it was in my father's day – got up all sorts of petitions and in the end the opposition was too strong. The cricket club survived, and although it's been through a couple of bad patches it's now as strong as it has ever been.'

'Thanks to you, it seems,' said Fanshawe.

'That's what people say,' said Sam Thatcher, unabashed. 'It's nice of them, but if people didn't want it, the club wouldn't exist. I just put all I've got into it, and, believe me, I get back just as much as I put in. Look at today's match. You couldn't have had a better afternoon; twenty-two men – beg pardon, twenty-one and a girl – out there battling away for more than five hours. Nearly four hundred runs. No-one hurt. And a finish within five minutes of time. Probably fifty or more people watching as well. What an afternoon's entertainment. For everybody, mind. Not just me.'

He related how a couple of weeks previously a newspaper man from London had come down to Brocester to do a story on the Village Cricket Championship, in a match which Brocester had lost. He'd brought his wife for the weekend out. 'They stayed in the pub here and went to church on the Sunday and there were twenty people there, including the parson. That afternoon, across the way, there were two thousand people watching the cricket match, and the coaches were lined up across the grass. The club bar took over £500 that night. It does treble that when we hold our brewing festival. You've seen the artificial pitch; that's meant the county play quite a lot of their Colts matches here, and that in turn's brought on our own junior sides. Phil Shaw here runs an under-eleven coaching session every Tuesday. On Wednesday Ploddy takes off his sergeant's stripes and runs an under-thirteen side. We've got several fifteen-year-olds down at the county nets at Easter, and there's even talk of starting up a girl's side. Though I don't know if your Gillian won't have all the girls trying to play properly with the men, like her.' He shook his head. 'I don't know if it's right. But she did all right, your girl.'

Their girl put her head round the door. 'Come on you old fogeys,' she said. 'Come and join in. It's the over-forties versus the under-forties. Losers pay for the drinks.' Thatcher declined, preferring to stay with Fanshawe, who no-one could really see scoring heavily at a game of skittles, but Gauvinier, nettled at being described as an 'old fogey', sank his pint and joined in with a will. After the over-forties and under-forties, it was girls versus men, with Gillian joining the Thatcher girls and their Brocester friends; and then Brocester v. Tillingfold, no holds barred and skittles crashing in all directions.

Promptly at eleven the landlord called, 'Time, ladies and gentlemen please,' to a chorus of dissent, and Sam Thatcher held up his hand.

'Don't worry everybody. It's time to move over to the club. The missus is there with a bite to eat for all; and because we don't want to get Ploddy here in any trouble, there won't be a bar. But seeing as it's Tillingfold's first visit, we thought we'd have a party, and I shouldn't be surprised if there's not a drop or two of punch to keep you warm.'

As they crossed the recreation ground in the warm night an enticing smell wafted across from the direction of the pavilion. On reaching its source, they found Mrs Thatcher presiding over two lengthy barbecue braziers, hung all over with chops and chicken-legs and sausages, with about a hundredweight of charcoal glowing white-red underneath.

Gauvinier's stomach reminded him how hungry he'd been, as the teams, whooping with delight, descended on the feast like a plague of locusts. One of the Thatcher girls gave Gauvinier a mug of steaming punch, and he wondered if it would mingle with the quantities of beer he had drunk earlier. He was never quite sure, because the rest of the evening passed in a cheerful haze. He remembered some time later finding himself dancing close to Gillian, with the club's disco blaring into the night and drowning whatever they tried to say to each other. He remembered being 'excused' by the eldest Thatcher girl – the one who'd given them the punch – and being dragged by her into what seemed to be a mixture of the Lancer and the latest break-dance; and of collapsing into a convenient chair while the noise and the sound boomed around him. And later still, he recovered his breath and his senses enough to wander out into the balmy night to breathe in the fresh air; to look back at the brightly-lit pavilion which seemed to expand and contract to the beat of the music and the thumping of feet. He found his way to the coach and climbed slowly into it, taking the nearest seat and letting himself relax, replete with beer and punch and barbecued meat, and longing suddenly for Polly and home and bed. A deep voice greeted him.

'Hello, Peter.'

Gauvinier looked across the aisle. It had to be Fanshawe, and Gauvinier felt guilty that he'd forgotten the umpire.

'Hello, Oliver. Are you all right?'

'I'm well, Peter. And you?'

'I have drink taken. It's time for bed.'

'It'll be some time yet before the rest of them agree with you,' said Fanshawe drily. 'D'you think it's going well?'

'I was going to ask you that,' said Gauvinier. 'You're the observer. I'd like to end the tour with a win, though.'

'That damned girl of yours is pulling her weight. And she's less trouble than I thought she'd be'. It was an admission, and a generous one.

'You still don't approve, though, wholly?'

He felt his friend smile in the darkness.

'Approve or not, you've got to move with the times. She's sweet on you though, Peter.'

That old-fashined phrase jolted Gauvinier. It was what Polly had said. He hastened to deny it.

'You must be joking, Oliver,' he said. 'I'm old enough to be her father.'

Fanshawe's voice was teasing.

'Don't you believe it. You're just the right age.'

'Don't be daft,' said Gauvinier, sharply. 'I wouldn't let it happen. I couldn't let it happen. It would wreck the club. It would spoil everything we've done these past few years.'

'You might not be able to stop it happening.'

Gauvinier, wide awake and angry, got up abruptly and jumped down from the coach, striding across the grass to clear his head and his thoughts. He could face the possibility that he might be attracted by Gillian's physical charms and outgoing personality. He could cope with that, suppress it if you like. He didn't think that she was the sort of girl to throw them around lightly. But what if she were to – his mind balked – fall in love with him? What to do then? Then what would happen to his good resolutions for himself, and his principled stance on behalf of Tillingfold? He got back into the coach.

'No, Oliver,' he said firmly. 'It hasn't happened. It won't happen. And I don't want to hear another word about it.'

But he resolved to pre-empt 'anything' happening. He would have a word with Gillian in the morning. When his head was clear. When both their heads were clear. He dropped off to sleep.

He was awakened by a crowd of singing voices and the clatter of happy bodies tumbling back into the coach. One plumped itself down beside him. It smelt of punch and barbecue sauce. It kissed him. On the lips. It was Gillian.

'Hullo, Guv,' she said comfortably, snuggling up beside him and laying her head on his shoulder, her curls against his cheek. 'I've been looking for you everywhere. I love you.' She hiccupped slightly and fell asleep. He hadn't the heart to wake her until the coach arrived back at the motel and they tumbled out, half asleep. Gauvinier got her key for her and turned it in the door, pushing her through it. He watched her drop sleepily onto the bed, said, 'Good night, Gill,' and then gently closed the door. He went to his own bed feeling both virtuous and foolish. It was a lonely night, and Fanshawe's sardonic eye over breakfast made him feel no better.

But what he said to Gillian, and Gillian said to him, when he went to her room at six o'clock in the morning, was not recorded in the annals of Tillingfold's tour.

Chapter Six

AFTER THE WARMTH and friendliness of Gloucestershire and Somerset, the Tillingfold travellers, intrepid though they no doubt felt they were, were little prepared for the harshness of the Cornish countryside. High on the moors, they travelled for mile upon mile across a nearly barren landscape, through the ghosts of little villages and past the ruins of old mine workings abandoned long ago. Trewartha, when they came upon it, was little more than a collection of stone houses – 'more like huts than houses' – lying tucked in to the side of the road, each made of the grey granite, with roofs slated in grey too, so that the whole melted into the landscape. A lone low public house declared forbiddingly 'No Coaches', and next to it a village store and post office displayed a number of faded posters for long-forgotten amateur dramatic shows and the sign: 'Closed until 2 p.m.'

Hunter pulled back his glass sliding window and questioned two small boys kicking stones along a gutter on the far side of the road.

'Can you tell us where the cricket club is?' he called in his most encouraging voice. 'Trewartha Cricket Club?'

'Down by yer,' and a jerked thumb indicated a side turning, and Hunter gingerly headed the coach down a road lined with the same stone cottages and a grey Methodist Chapel with no apparent windows and a bare stone cross fronting its low roof. Unexpectedly, they spotted a small, clean notice: 'Trewartha Cricket Club', with an arrow somewhat confusingly pointing in the diametrically opposite direction to another arrow which said, obligingly: 'Cricket Field'. Hunter turned the coach towards the arrow pointing to the club and a few seconds later pulled up on a wide roughly rolled-out car park by a long low building. Over a small door was the notice: 'Trewartha CC'.

Gauvinier pushed open the door and paused in astonishment. Laid out before his eyes was one of the biggest, most plush bars he had seen outside the West End. In contrast to the chill wind outside, it was centrally heated to the point of suffocation. Low tables were set out, with long settees and easy chairs for at least a hundred people. On his left a well-stocked bar could cater for a small army of drinkers; and a young battery of electronic bandits and space-age games were lined up against one wall. A small, dark man with long sideburns and a thick moustache peeled himself from the bar and came forward.

'Are you Tillingfold?' he asked in an accent echoing that of the small boys in the street. 'Come in and help yourselves, boys. Drinks on the house, of course.' He shook hands all round, introducing himself.

'I'm the secretary. The skipper and the club president will be down in a minute to meet you. We didn't expect you for another hour or so. My name's Taylor, Gordon Taylor.'

Mitterman did the honours for Tillingfold. He

was good at that sort of thing.

'I'm James Mitterman, Tillingfold secretary. I was the one who wrote to you. This is Peter Gauvinier, our captain.' He went round the team, most of them furnished with pints of bitter from the bar. Gauvinier, mindful of Wym, chose an orange juice. He commented on the size of the clubhouse to Mr Taylor.

'Ah yes, it's all due to the recession,' said the secretary. He pointed to a large fading team photograph on the wall. There, you see, that was our champion team of 1922. You'll see there were four Taylors in it, and three Turners. My father was captain then. Now there are four Turners and three Taylors in the Trewartha team, and they're all grandchildren of those old folks in the picture.'

He then pointed to a modern coloured photograph.

'That's last year's team, practically the same as this year's. You see: there's the Turners, sitting in a row. That's Jack, the captain, with the bat, and Harry, and Ned and Arthur: and the Taylors are in the back row. The biggest lad in the middle is John, my son.'

'That's quite a record,' said Gauvinier. There were names in the Tillingfold scorebook still which also appeared on the stone cross commemorating two World Wars, and there was a Parish record of a Gauvinier who had fought in the Crimea; but nothing as impressive as this. 'But that doesn't explain the size of the club.'

'Ah, you see,' said Mr Taylor earnestly, 'It's the recession. It's the second time it's happened. You've seen all the old mine-heads around?'

Gauvinier nodded.

'Well, this part of Cornwall lived for centuries on the tin and the copper; and Trewartha Jane was the biggest mine in these parts. Then in the twenties nobody wanted copper or tin any more, and the mines went out of business. There are about two thousand, five hundred people in Trewartha, and by 1919 there were over six hundred out of work. The only thing that kept the village going was the old cricket club. People would turn out – five hundred or a thousand on a Saturday – to see Trewartha play the best teams in the county.

'And then the war came – the second war I mean – and some of the mines went back into business. The International Mining Company opened up here, and by the fifties there were more than four thousand men employed at the factory just over the hill. They weren't all from the village, of course, but Trewartha was prosperous again. Now they're back to employing under a thousand men, and we've over twenty-five per cent unemployment in the village. But the cricket club's still here, and expanding. It holds the village together. It's taken over from the church and the old WI. The women hold their meetings here now since their hut began to leak. And we're still getting up to a thousand at the matches on Saturday – you'll have quite a few hundred this afternoon, I shouldn't wonder. They like to see Trewartha win.'

'I don't know about that,' Gauvinier smiled, 'but we'll give you a good game.' He looked at the pictures on the wall again. The men all appeared to be dark and small, and very similar in appearance. He commented on the family likenesses.

'Oh yes,' said Mr Taylor, 'We're all birds of a feather down here. Been breeding for so long, you know.'

He showed them round the club, pointing out the features with some pride. Trewartha boasted a second 'cocktail' bar, and a large games room sporting two full-size billiard tables and table tennis.

'Of course there's darts. That's very popular, particularly since it's been on television,' said Mr Taylor. 'Snooker too. It gives the men something to do during the day and when it rains.'

Gauvinier asked: 'But how does the club keep going financially, with so many people out of work round here?'

'Oh, we're all right there.' He pointed to the two electronic gambling machines. 'They keep us going. We take £10,000 profit out of each one of those each year. We built the clubhouse ourselves, every bit, and the company provided us with the land at a peppercorn rent. The cricket field's ours, too, and we've just put up a new scoreboard which is good enough for county matches. 'Aye, Tests too I wouldn't be surprised,' he added proudly. 'Come up and see for yourselves. We've time before the girls get the lunch for you.'

He led them along the short walk to the cricket field, which stood slightly higher than the rest of the village and, although the sun was shining, they immediately felt exposed to the cool breeze.

'Ah,' said Mr Taylor. 'It can get mighty chilly of an evening here.' He pointed to the scoreboard, a brick-built construction of imposing size. 'You couldn't do better than that.'

The Tillingfold players were impressed. Their own scoreboard, like that of most village clubs, was a primitive affair consisting of a blackboard with a series of nails, and a little box full of metal plates with numbers on them. There had been considerable embarrassment during one match when there were insufficient figures for the score eighty-eight, eight, eight to be put up. Such a misfortune would obviously not occur at Trewartha.

Gauvinier looked around the horizon. Even in the sunlight, it was bleak, with a forlorn mine-head breaking the monotony. There were no trees, everything seemed to have been scoured by the wind. The cricket field itself was beautifully tended, as well as that at Brocester, except that the dry summer had slightly scorched the outfield grass. The square itself was immaculate, with a freshly-mown wicket newly marked out and the stumps lying ready for the umpires to set in their holes. Trewartha followed the strict tradition: the umpires should pitch the wickets, not the groundsman. The fine grass was marked here and there – even on the square – with irregular dark-green circles, which Gauvinier remembered from his childhood as 'fairy rings'. He commented on them to Mr Taylor and another dark, moustachioed figure who had joined them.

'They don't make any difference to the pitch.' The groundsman sounded truculent, as though Gauvinier was criticising.

Gauvinier hastened to reassure him. 'I wondered what caused them.'

The groundsman launched himself into a complicated explanation of the mineral components of the Cornish subsoil, but finishing: 'We don't rightly know', and Gauvinier was left with fairy rings. He hoped the Trewartha bowlers weren't magicians, too.

He had one slightly tricky psychological problem to solve, which in one way was welcome. Trewartha were by reputation certainly the strongest of all the four teams they faced on their tour, but the professional approach and appearance of the ground had surprised Gauvinier, who in consequence wanted to play the strongest possible Tillingfold side against them. The day's rest and the combined care of the Thatcher girls at Brocester had worked wonders with Norman Smith's finger, and he had solemnly declared himself fit to play. Richard Veysey's back was still causing him problems, so he was unavailable. Which meant leaving out one of the players who had performed against Brocester. In fairness, it could not be either Budgeon or Bewers, both of whom had played in only one match so far on the tour. Gillian's bowling was going to be essential; Frank'n'Fred were indispensable members of the side. So were White and Jess, the crack batsmen. There was no other wicketkeeper, although Trine had on occasions donned the gloves; but Joe Deacon was an essential part of his plans. Which left either Trine or Mitterman. Gauvinier would dearly have loved to leave out James, who was but a poor cricketer, but as he had organised the tour, was to miss the last match for business reasons and would certainly take badly to being dropped, Gavuinier did not want to rock the Tillingfold boat. Mitterman was too useful a club member to offend, and although Gauvinier despised himself for bowing to such considerations, he had long ago learned that a little compromise goes a long way to keep a club ticking over harmoniously.

He brooded over the problem during Trewartha's lunch, which was a rather indigestible mixture of hot Cornish pasties and baked potatoes in their jackets, and eventually took the easy way out.

'Teddy, I'm going to have to ask you to stand down this afternoon,' he said, taking Trine aside after lunch. 'I'm in a bit of a spot. I've got to play Norman now he's fit, because Trewartha's obviously a strong side, and I've got to leave someone out.

Trine grinned. 'You don't have to spell it out, Guv. It's either me or Sunny Jim there. I've been dying to get my hands on that new scoreboard of theirs. Don't worry about a thing. I've had a great tour. And any way, Quim – you remember Quincey? – said she'd drive down here today. So long as you don't mind going to Devon one short in the coach. Don't give it another thought.'

Gauvinier, mortified by the young man's easy good nature and still feeling guilty, bustled away self-consciously to organise the carrying of gear from the coach to the little pavilion. The changing rooms and showers were all in the clubhouse itself; the pavilion was used as a shelter for kit and against sudden squalls or rain, not uncommon, Mr Taylor said, in Cornwall, even in such fine weather as this.

It was astonishing, Gauvinier thought, how the Cornishmen conformed to type. Jack Turner, the Trewartha captain, who had dark long sideburns and dark brown eyes like most of his team, and stood three inches shorter than Gauvinier's 5 ft 11 ins, proferred one explanation. 'It's to fool our visitors,' he said. 'They never know which one of us is in and which is out. The scorers have a bit of a problem. But don't worry. My brother – that's young Ken – is the scorer, and he knows us all. We don't cheat down here. Only fairly.'

'I'm glad to hear it,' said Gauvinier. 'And I suppose you have the fairies bowling for you too?' He pointed to the green rings in the grass.

'Ah, I don't think the fairies favour us one little bit this year,' said Taylor. 'We lost more than we've won, and we were put out of the Whitbread championship in the second round – the first time we've done so badly.

Still, perhaps they'll be on our side today. Call.'

He spun the coin, and Gauvinier, daring the fairies, varied his usual call and said 'Tails'. And won the toss.

'You bat,' he said without hesitation. He would attack.

There are games when for one reason or another, or no reason at all, every ball is memorable. The Tillingfold-Trewartha match was just such a one for Gauvinier at least, and for some of the more sensitive Tillingfold players. Trewartha would remember it too, for it was one of those games that came to life not only for the players, but also for the several hundred spectators who gathered round the low stone walls surrounding the field. There were performances on both sides, not to put too fine a point on it, that had epic proportions; there were one or two instances of sportsmanship that grace the very best of cricket matches, and, as Gauvinier and Fanshawe reflected afterwards, every single member of the Tillingfold side contributed. Even James Mitterman. But they didn't win.

Norman Smith began it, bowling at his fastest down the slope from the pavilion end. He forgot his damaged finger at once and struck a beautiful length. The two Turners, Ned and Arthur, who opened the Trewartha batting, acknowledged in the bar afterwards that they had rarely faced a more hostile opening spell. Moving the ball seemingly at will, off the seam or in the air, Norman kept them both guessing and prodding, fending off balls which reared and ducked and swerved and swung, until eventually Ned got the faintest of touches outside the off stump and Deacon, with a roar that could have been heard in Truro, leapt into the air with the ball securely held in both gloves.

'HAAAT!'

'Out,' said the Trewartha umpire, raising his finger. And Ned trudged back to the pavilion, passing Norman on his way and muttering: 'Well bowled.'

At the other end, Bill Budgeon had caused gasps of astonishment around the boundary when he began to bowl, with his shuffling cripple's run-up and smoothly-flowing arm action. At the end of his first over, a maiden, the crowd applauded, for every ball had pitched on a length and forced the batsman to play, or to play and miss, the ball smacking into Deacon's gloves with a satisfactory 'thwack'. Gauvinier felt the whole team was on its toes, willing itself forward as one man, keyed up for the slightest chance. And when it came, it was Budgeon who gave it expression.

Norman Smith, having conceded only ten runs in his first five overs for one wicket, was rested by Gauvinier. Instead of putting himself on he threw the ball to Gillian. 'Shock tactics,' he said. 'They don't know what to expect.'

And indeed, although the batsmen tried to look suspicious at the thought of a girl bowling to them, Gauvinier felt rather than saw a relaxation in their attitudes. Arthur Turner, who had presented the dourest of straight bats to all Norman's best endeavours, took a dive at an offensive daisy while Gillian set her field, and his partner selected a new piece of grass to chew. Gauvinier settled himself at slip, and moved Budgeon a little wider into a short gully position.

Gillian made up for her lack of height and pace with a subtlety of approach that was not always appreciated, both within Tillingfold and without. Her stock ball was a medium-paced inswinger, which she tried to 'straighten' off the pitch. By varying her grip on the ball, shifting her middle finger from one side of the seam to the other, she was able occasionally to produce one that 'went the other way', specifically an outswinger which could, on her good days, cut back sharply. She was aided by the fact that she herself never knew which type of grip was going to take effect. When she had confessed this to Gauvinier and Fanshawe, she had been much comforted by Fanshawe's: 'Ah, that's the best sort of bowling. If you don't know what you're going to produce, then how on earth can the batsman find out?'

As usual, she began by bowling her inswinger, as she knew it. And as sometimes happened it turned out to be an outswinger, slightly short of a length, which cut back off the pitch. Arthur Turner, his foot across and raised for the square cut as he found the ball short and swinging away, suddenly discovered the ball a foot nearer to him than he had been expecting. Judging it still to be of hittable speed and height, he went through with the stroke, in normal circumstances a well-hit square cut 'in the meat' of the bat and winging its way towards the boundary wide of Budgeon's right hand at gully. But instead of skimming the turf, the ball was a foot off the ground, and Budgeon's great right hand swooped out and held it as he crashed painfully onto his crippled right knee and landed on his back. The field echoed with applause.

'Jesus,' was all the astounded batsman could think of. But he walked over and helped Budgeon to his feet: 'That was the best catch I've ever seen,' he said as Tillingfold joined the crowd in appreciation of his sportsmanship. And Budgeon stood shyly, acknowledging the applause and gently clapping his hands to the retreating batsman's back.

'Are you all right, Bill?' Gauvinier inquired anxiously. He did not want his bowler hurt.

Budgeon flexed various muscles and winced.

'Be all right today. Be a bit sore tomorrow,' he grinned. 'I'll remember that'un.'

'And so will I, Bill,' Gauvinier added sincerely.

At fifteen for two, with the bowlers well on top, it seemed the game had swung early in Tillingfold's favour. But Trewartha were made of sterner stuff. At the crease were Jack Turner, the skipper, and his first cousin, Harry; and they fought their way out of the trough with character and good cricket. For all their similarity in appearance, they had contrasting styles at the wicket. Where Jack bustled about, using his feet to advance up the wicket to drive, lying right back to cut and sweep, Harry maintained a calm uprightness, apparently imperturbable, but driving with withering force whenever a ball was over-pitched. He was particularly severe on Gillian, whom Gauvinier took off after five overs for her one wicket and twenty-four runs. In her place he gave himself a turn, quickly finding a length and keeping the batsmen quiet for long spells, even though they both prospered at the other end.

It was Frank Hunter, with his unpredictable leg-breaks who broke the stand after the pair had put on eighty runs. Harry Turner, the driver, swung once too often as Frank got the ball to turn and lift, and Paul White took a swirling catch at cover. The crowd applauded Harry, a great favourite, all the way back to the pavilion, and settled back to see Jack and his new partner, a burly young man who looked as though he meant business, take the Tillingfold bowling apart.

But it didn't happen. Gauvinier, with one of those inspired changes of plan he couldn't explain, even in retrospect, brought Norman Smith back on to bowl, uphill from the bottom end this time, and switched himself to the pavilion end. Suddenly Trewartha were in all sorts of trouble.

After a long stand, it is not unusual for one partner to follow the other back to the pavilion comparatively quickly. Maybe it has something to do with the release of tension; or maybe the fielding side is inspired to extra effort by the fall of a wicket. In any event, Gauvinier could sense new purpose in his team as Norman ran in to bowl. The ball lifted sharply off the pitch and Jack Turner, surprised into a quick defensive push, found the ball careering high off the shoulder of his bat towards the second slip position. Gillian, moving smoothly to her left, took the ball at shoulder height with both hands, swinging round with the pace of the ball and throwing it aloft in excitement. A hundred and three, four, sixty read the scoreboard. Within ten minutes it was a hundred and ten, six, two as Gauvinier took a wicket, nicely stumped down the leg side by Deacon, and Norman sent the number six batsman's off stump cartwheeling. Budgeon caught the ball high over his head in the gully.

Dixon, a capable-looking young man, had stood for some while at the bowler's end of the pitch, watching these disasters with a growing expression of gloom, not to say bad temper. When he eventually faced the bowling he gave expression to his mood by hitting Norman Smith for three fours in one over, and then planting Gauvinier over his head for two sixes.

Enough is enough, thought Gauvinier, and switched his bowling again. Gillian promptly took another wicket, bowling the Trewartha number eight batsman with one that cut back 'through the gate' of an inexperienced defensive stroke.

A hundred and forty for seven wickets rapidly became a hundred and seventy for eight as the belligerent young man dusted up his square cutting and raced to his fifty with a vast pull which threatened the construction of the new scorebox. Gauvinier put a stop to all that and bowled him across a similar pull, calculating that, as so often happens, a man who will pull a perfectly good length ball for six will hit clean across a half-volley. Deacon, who had been waiting for the stumping as the batsman was a yard out of his ground, called cheerfully to Gauvinier: 'I knew we'd get him, Guv,' making little movements of his gloves as though flicking off the bails.

'I didn't need you that time, Joe.'

'Ah, but I was there, Guv.'

It was now twenty minutes to five and Tillingfold, still on their toes, set out to capture the last two wickets. A stubborn little stand developed for the ninth wicket, the batsmen edging ones and twos and the occasional four before Norman took a simple caught and bowled, a hundred and eighty-five for nine. A hundred and eighty-five all out as Norman swept away the last man's defences with his next ball. Tillingfold, and Gauvinier, had every reason to be pleased with themselves, if a little tired, as the players went in to their tea. Norman Smith, as befits one who had taken five wickets for fifty runs, led the way in.

From somewhere an ice-cream van had pulled up at the gates, doing roaring business during the tea interval, while the more provident spectators brought out thermos flasks and sipped at hot tea or coffee while wondering how soon the wind was going to turn really cold.

After tea it was Tillingfold's turn. The tough young man who had scored fifty turned out to be a roly-poly sort of fast bowler who, like Norman Smith, could bowl clean through an innings, and in fact did so from the pavilion end, taking wickets and conceding runs with compensating generosity. Turner, the skipper, took a longish, medium-pace spell from the other end, but Gauvinier was relieved to find that the home side did not appear to have a slow spin bowler. Trewartha compensated for this lack by fielding like demons, saving at least forty runs in the field as each side in turn tried to establish its superiority.

Jess and Mitterman opened for Tillingfold, but Jess was soon out, playing across a perfectly straight ball from Dixon, the burly young man, and being bowled for only three runs. Mitterman, however, uncharacteristically put down what appeared to be a reasonably safe anchor at one end, staying in for over three quarters of an hour while Paul White played one of his most dazzling knocks at the other end. When White was out at last, brilliantly caught for forty-four at second slip, again off Dixon, Mitterman was still there with thirteen runs to his credit; and the score had reached sixty-five for two.

Honours even so far, thought Gauvinier, as he picked up his batting gloves and strode out to the wicket. 'Well done, James, keep it up,' he told Mitterman, who came to greet him with the not too helpful news that 'that chap at the top end wants watching,' but unfortunately did not follow his own advice, for a few balls later he played back to a ball of full length and was plumb, palpably lbw.

Gauvinier applauded him as he walked past on the way to the pavilion. 'Good knock, James,' and indeed the secretary had played a sterling role in tiring the Trewartha bowlers. The next man in, Bobby Bewers, took guard and flicked airily at his first ball, which swept fast and low to the left of the short fine leg, who dived desperately to come up holding the ball aloft. Abashed, Bobby began to walk back to the pavilion but the fielder tossed the ball back to the wicketkeeper. 'Stay there, young'un,' he called. 'I grounded it. T'was no catch.' But the escape did not profit Bewers or Tillingfold. Bobby swung hard at the next ball again and, getting the thinnest of edges, was easily caught by the tough young wicketkeeper. He did not have to appeal, as Bewers was walking even before the ball was in the keeper's hands. 'Sorry, Guv,' he said as he passed Gauvinier. 'Rush of blood.' Gauvinier nodded sadly. The fight was on.

Frank Hunter stopped with him for a few overs; so did Fred Bason. Gauvinier was beginning to feel a fixture in the middle, but was beginning to eye the clock on the pavilion with misgivings and the scoreboard with even less cheer. One hundred for six wickets and an hour to go (or twenty overs, he reminded himself). To score eighty-six runs to win was a tall order for the bottom half of the Tillingfold team. Gauvinier took a fresh guard and a fresh hold on his determination as Gillian joined him at the crease. There was no relaxing on the part of Trewartha. They bowled like furies and fielded like demons, but the skipper and the girl kept out their best deliveries and gradually forced the home side onto the defence.

Jack Turner was forced to take two of his three slips away. One was sent down to third man, where Gillian had steered two fours; the other went out to extra cover to block Gauvinier's favourite shot, the drive, which was beginning to sting the hands of the offside field. One hundred crept to a hundred and ten; a hundred and twenty came up slowly; a hundred and thirty a little faster and suddenly, after a three from Gillian and two creaking fours from Gauvinier, the hundred and fifty was on the board. Thirty-six runs to win and eight overs left to get them in. Gauvinier began to feel the game might be nearly safe; but the tables suddenly turned with one of those mishaps that can only happen at cricket.

Gillian drove a ball from Dixon hard and precisely straight down the pitch. The bowler, who ran in a wide arc and who followed through well to the offside of the wicket, dived desperately to stop a certain four. His fingertips touched the ball which rolled onto the wicket, leaving Gauvinier, following up, stranded a yard down the wicket, unable to turn to make his ground. Miserable though it was, there was no relief. Gauvinier was out, as out as he would have been had he been clean bowled. Run out for fifty-nine; and now Tillingfold had three wickets to fall and were still thirty-six runs short of victory.

Gillian took a grip on her feelings. There was no use crying over spilt milk. Tillingfold would either win or they wouldn't, and she knew the run-out had been one of those diabolical pieces of luck. It had not been her fault, though she could still feel aggrieved like any batsman that a certain four had instead led to a vital wicket for the opposition. She gritted her teeth and cut Dixon's next ball for four runs, bisecting gully and third man and bringing a cheer from Gauvinier, who forgot to take his pads off and sat the rest of the game alternately chewing his batting gloves and thumping his bat on the ground in excitement.

No more runs were scored off that over, and Norman Smith was in to face the bowling. Thirty-two runs to go; three wickets to fall; seven overs left. Now Turner, the captain, was back on bowling, the fieldsmen clustered round the bat. Norman stepped down the wicket and swung the ball high into the outfield. Safe. Two runs, three as Gillian forced the pace from the easy two runs and they came home – just – on Arthur Turner's very good throw to the keeper. Gillian glanced the next ball for a single down to fine leg, one that they shouldn't have turned into two, but fine-leg tossed the ball back too casually high in the air. Shouting, 'Come on, Norman,' at the top of her voice, Gillian scrambled home again. Cheers and some laughter from the crowd, who had given her some good natured banter when she went in to bat, but had taken to her skill and bravery. She blocked the next three balls, digging the last, a vicious yorker, out of the blockhole at the last second.

'Well played, lass,' said the keeper as he passed her at the end of the over, giving her shoulder a friendly pat. Norman grinned at her down the pitch: 'It's fun, this, isn't it?' and hit the next ball tremendously high so it took an age to come down. One of the Taylors was underneath it, however, and pray as they might, he held the swirling ball as it descended from the heavens as though it were a nursery balloon. Twenty-seven runs to go now, but only two wickets to fall and fewer than six overs left. Joe Deacon took Norman's place and the Trewartha skipper called the entire team round the batsman, apart from third man and one player out at mid-off. Turner bowled. Deacon blocked. Turner bowled, Deacon missed, the wicketkeeper grabbed and third man had to run a long way to stop the boundary byes as the batsmen ran two. Turner bowled again. Deacon played and missed to a half-stifled shout from one of the slips. Turner bowled. Deacon stopped it.

Now it was Dixon's turn again, straining every muscle to dismiss this slip of a girl who stood between Trewartha and victory. She could do little but block defensively the first four balls, but when he strayed, on the fifth ball, down the leg side, she swung the ball hard and true to the long-leg boundary. Dixon dug the last ball of the over in short, trying for a bouncer. Gillian, tensely alert for every trick, saw it coming and moved inside the line of the ball, letting it whistle harmlessly through to the wicketkeeper. 'Aim at the stumps, Dicko,' came from round the ground. Twenty-one runs to go. Four overs left. Two wickets to fall.

And now only one; for Deacon had prodded and not missed, but popped the ball up, a simple little catch to one of the six fielders gathered close round the bat, and the fielder, in his anxiety, had let it pop up out of his hands not once but twice, clutching it to his bosom at the third attempt, to the relief of his team-mates and ironical applause from the boundary. The ripple for the last man hardly disturbed the tension as Budgeon made his awkward way to the wicket, pad on his left leg but nothing on his crippled right. No batting gloves, and his old bat, dark like a piece of mahogany and bound round with the tape of ages. There was a grin on his rubicund Sussex face. 'We can do it, Missy. None of that fancy running now.' And Gillian laughed and promised, only to be taken by surprise when Budgeon belted the first ball he received, hitting silly point on the ankle and forcing her to take a very quick single as the ball cannoned out into the covers. Gillian, taking advantage of the cluster of fielders round the bat, cut the next ball prettily almost out of the hands of first slip, through his legs and racing away to the boundary; and Jack Turner came to his senses and redistributed his forces. This girl had proved she could score runs; but she made no more off the over, which left Tillingfold needing sixteen runs to win with three overs left.

They so nearly did it. Budgeon hit one four, a flat-batted, baseball type hit off Dixon which screamed for four past point's head with all the close fielders cowering. Gillian drove Turner for a three and faced the last over needing nine runs to win with every Trewartha fielder crouched round the bat. Undaunted, she stepped out to the first ball and hit it over the leg side field for four. The Tillingfold team jumped to their feet as one man to applaud the stroke, and quite a number of the spectators were standing now too. She tried again, but this time the ball flew off the inside edge of the bat for a single. Budgeon could do nothing with the third ball, but shuffled down the wicket to the fourth and scrambled a leg bye, the umpire turning a blind eye to appeals for lbw.

Three to win; two balls to go. Gillian kept out a brute of a ball and somehow kept it down, but no runs came. Budgeon edged up the wicket. A four would settle it; could they run a three?

As the bowler advanced, so did Gillian, two paces down the pitch. He saw her coming and prepared to pitch short outside the off stump, where the wicket-keeper was poised, waiting for the stumping. As the bowler's arm came over she stepped quickly back in the crease and cut the ball square into the cover field. Cover point, diving desperately, got a hand to the ball, half stopping it. The batsmen ran. The fielder scrambled to his feet and chased after the ball. Third man came round the boundary to cut it off and flicked the ball up cleanly to his colleague who had the better arm. Gillian and Budgeon had started on their third run – the winning run – but the fielder's throw ripped into the wicketkeeper's gloves with the limping Budgeon still half way down the pitch. The match was over. It was a tie, and the players were cheered from the field.

Afterwards, in the dressing room, Gillian discovered that her second run off the last ball had brought her her fifty – the first half-century she had ever made for any team, even in girl's cricket. But that knowledge failed to assuage her disappointment that the match had not been won.

'That was a real match, that was,' Turner said, shaking Gauvinier by the hand and seeking out Gillian. 'By God, I never thought I'd see a girl play cricket like that.' And the Tillingfold players gathered round, vying with Trewartha to congratulate her. The disappointment slowly turned into a satisfying glow, which even included Paul White, whose usually cynical young face shone with enthusiasm. 'Ain't she great?' he kept asking everyone. 'Ain't she just bloody great?'

Neither Gauvinier nor Fanshawe could recall a Tillingfold tie before, but both agreed that for excitement and achievement the game had made the whole tour worthwhile. And that evening, in the plush Trewartha Clubhouse, they were treated to sausages and mashed potatoes and a session of community singing not to be bettered outside a Welsh rugby club. 'Oh yes,' said Jack Turner. 'We Cornish can sing. Even if we can't play cricket.'

'Come off it, Jack.' (They were all on first name terms by now.) 'You bloody nearly beat us.'

'Ay, and *you* bloody nearly beat us.' But they all agreed that there could have been no more satisfactory outcome, nor a more exciting match.

Some time after midnight, they piled their gear wearily back into the coach and Frank Hunter drove them, with several stops for natural relief on the way, back towards Exeter, where at three in the morning they found their motel, and woke up a dozing clerk to give them the keys of their rooms. Gillian slept the whole way, knowing nothing of the stops, a small smile at the corner of her lips.

Chapter Seven

IT WAS PROBABLY inconceivable, said Gauvinier later, that a party of fourteen could go through a five-day tour without some form of bust-up. And it was also most likely to happen after a long and tiring night. The weary tourists assembled at breakfast later that morning feeling the anticlimax of the previous day's game, and quite daunted at the prospect of a fourth match that afternoon. Their tempers were not improved by finding that the self-service food was of the all-purpose plastic variety, with the eggs displaying a rubber quality which matched the cold toast and the congealing bacon. Gillian turned over some scambled egg which had the consistency of emulsion paint with a shudder and settled for a glass of (synthetic) orange juice and a cup of black coffee. Her head felt thick and her muscles ached, and from the attitude of the rest of the team she felt sure they were all suffering from similar symptoms.

An exception seemed to be Paul White, who was busily finishing off a huge plate of eggs and bacon, garnished with a greasy mixture which Gillian diagnosed to be fried mushrooms and tomatoes. As his method of eating used the knife and fork as a continuous conveyor-belt to a mouth lowered over the plate, it was not a very edifying spectacle, but as the seat opposite him was the only one free that Gillian could occupy without seeming really rude, she sat down between Trine and Jess and sipped at her orange juice.

'How was the score box?' she asked Trine, more to distract her own attention than anything else. Trine, who was eating toast and marmalade and thinking deeply of the charms of one Quincey Wym, who indeed had driven to Trewartha and had promised to be at Clyst St Cob later that day as well, mumbled a reply. 'Oh . . . oh, it wasn't too uncomfortable.'

Across the table White wiped his mouth on his sleeve and sat back in his chair. His long legs under the table rubbed against Gillian's. He belched slightly.

'Come on, Teddy, you can do better than that,' he said. 'The lady wants to know what it was like sitting in the bleeding scorebox while she piled up her half-ton.'

Trine looked at him.

'Get back to your trough,' he said coldly. 'Miss Grantham was talking to me.'

'Ah, but she was playing kneesy with me,' said White, lighting a cigarette and blowing the smoke across the table. Gillian got to her feet.

'Excuse me,' she said, keeping her temper with an effort. 'I think I'll take my coffee to my room.'

'Our company not good enough for you?'

She looked at him. 'At breakfast, frankly, no.'

'Nor any other time,' said Trine, his usually amiable face reddening with anger.

'Oh, she's going to give you a turn, don't worry, after you've finished with your randy little piece of the peerage.'

'I'm not listening to any more of this,' said Gillian.

Jess laid a hand on her arm.

'Don't go,' he said gently, 'before Mr White apologises for being a loud-mouthed berk.'

Jess stood up and moved round the table. Trine made to get up to help him but Jess waved him back into his seat. 'It's all right, Teddy, I don't need any assistance, thank you.' He stood behind White's chair. 'Are you going to apologise to Gillian?' he said mildly. White half twisted in his seat and sneered at him. 'You and who else is going to fuckin' make me?'

Jess took the little finger of White's hand, the one that was holding the cigarette, and twisted it back sharply. With his other hand he grasped the lobe of White's left ear and twisted that too. White shot to his feet, face contorted but bent over like a small boy in the hands of a merciless schoolmaster. 'Let me go. You're hurting me,' he said furiously. Jess applied a little more pressure with both hands.

'You have something to say to Gillian,' he said, still mildly.

'Sorry.' It was a schoolboy's mumble.

'That's enough Albert, let him go.' Gauvinier did not want the incident to turn into anything worse. 'I want him this afternoon. And you Paul, just watch your language. You know I won't tolerate it. And while you're on tour you're part of the team. All right, everybody, the party's over. Let's get on with breakfast.'

'I've finished mine,' said White, and made for the door.

Trine looked at Jess with some respect.

'Where did you learn to do that?'

'Ah,' said Jess, who on occasions had had to use more subtle ways of fighting off the attentions of fans. 'Don't ask.'

'All right, I won't. Miss Grantham, as I was saying when we were so rudely interrupted, the scorebox was cold, draughty and most uncomfortable, but it worked very well. And would you care for another cup of coffee?'

Gillian laughed, and sat down, surrendering her cup. 'I will, yes please. It's gone cold, anyway.'

'What was wrong with that young man?' Bason had just come in. 'He passed me with a look as though he could have killed me.'

'Oh, I think he was fed up with being upstaged by Gillian here. After all, he had a darned good innings for his forty-four, only for little Gill to go and score fifty. She upstaged us all, in fact.'

The talk became general, and Paul White was forgotten. But Gillian knew that there was a mine of antagonism in the young man still to be faced. It was as though her presence in the team aroused a sexual aggression in him that was both unpleasant and totally rejectable.

The next outburst came from Frank Hunter, who had gone out to check on his coach. One of the rear tyres had gone flat overnight, which necessitated the tedious business of hauling out the jack, hoisting up the heavy vehicle and putting on the spare wheel. Fred Bason went out to help him, for it was far too heavy a job for one man, and they returned after an hour with scuffed knuckles and greasy clothes, neither in a particularly benign mood.

'What d'you mean, no coffee?' Hunter glared at the waitress who was clearing away the remains of breakfast.

'Sorry, sir, breakfast is finished.'

'I know that. All I want is a cup of coffee. I've been slaving my guts out there for the past hour and I want a cup of coffee. Go and get me one.'

'I'll get the manager,' the girl said hastily, for Frank, large and dirty, with a grease mark down the side of his face, was a menacing sight.

'And tell him to bring some coffee,' he shouted at her disappearing back.

The manager appeared, slim and suave and apologetic. But firm.

'I'm sorry sir, but this is a motel, not an hotel. We don't serve anything between mealtimes.'

Frank Hunter put a big hand up to his face and wiped off the sweat. Much of the grease came away on his palm. He looked at it and at the manager. He showed him the filthy hand.

'See that? And see your nice cream jacket? Go and tell that hoity-toity madam in the frills to bring me some coffee. Now!' he barked suddenly, and the manager, who was a prudent young man, jumped a foot and hastened away with, 'Oh, very well, sir,' thrown over his shoulder.

'And make sure it's hot.' Frank laughed. 'I feel better for that,' he said. 'Anyway, we're getting our coffee.' Bason, who had taken no part in the exchange, smiled slowly and answered: 'That's right, Frank,' and Hunter, suspicious as ever, looked at him under his brows and growled: 'And if I have any lip from you, I'll thump you as well.'

'Oh, no you won't,' said Fred calmly. 'Here's your coffee. Drink it up now before it gets cold. You made fuss enough to get it.' He sought out the waitress and gave her a generous tip. 'Don't worry, lass, we've had a bit of a morning.'

By eleven o'clock they were ready to move on. Gauvinier counted heads round the coach. Mitterman had left, picked up by a chauffer-driven Rolls Royce to attend a long-planned business meeting in Exeter. He would not play this afternoon, but would rejoin the party for the journey home afterwards. There were two people missing. Jess and White.

'Where the devil have they got to?' Gauvinier asked irritably, addressing his question to the coach in general. 'They can't still be scrapping, surely?'

'There's Jess!' said someone.

Jess came running across the tarmac, in his shirtsleeves.

'Peter,' he said urgently. 'My jacket's gone. Someone's pinched my jacket.'

'Are you sure it's not in your room?'

'Absolutely. I went back to the room to go to the loo and pick up my kit. I laid my jacket on the bed and went into the bathroom, and when I came out it had gone.'

'Was there anything in it? Wallet? Money?'

'Oh, the lot,' said Jess bitterly. 'Wallet, credit cards and about a hundred and fifty quid. I didn't even bother to shut the door. We'll have to get the police.'

'The trouble is,' said Gauvinier slowly. 'Paul White doesn't seem to be here either. We'd better look for him first.'

The coach was silent, as the team contemplated the obvious explanation.

'I don't believe it,' said Jess, heavily. 'He wouldn't do such a bloody silly thing. It's so . . . so . . . *BLOODY* silly.' He could find no more words.

'Come on,' said Gauvinier wearily, 'let's look for him.'

But a swift search of the few rooms revealed no sign of the missing White. Gauvinier went to the manager, and then reluctantly called the police. This was far beyond the worst he had contemplated could happen on the tour. The whole enterprise was soured. The players got down from the coach and sat moodily around in the motel's sparse lounge as they waited for the police. They all appeared more shaken than angry. Richard Veysey voiced their feelings.

'There's got to be some other explanation. I . . . we've all known Paul from a baby. I'm sure he wouldn't do anything so wicked.' The archaic word hung in the air.

They didn't have to wait long. Two brisk young policemen drove up in a panda car, explaining they'd been called on the radio from traffic duty.

'Don't worry, sir,' the elder of the two told Gauvinier. Gauvinier thought he looked about seventeen years old. 'We'll soon pick him up. You go on with your tour. Where are you going? Clyst St Cob? We'll be in touch.'

They marched back to their car, which slewed round in a flurry of engine revs and zoomed onto the main road. One policeman was already talking on his radio. Gauvinier felt sorry for Paul White. And for Tillingfold. Jess, strangely, who had lost his property, was the most cheerful among them as they slowly got back into the coach.

'It was only an old jacket, anyway,' he said. 'And I can claim the money from my insurance company. I've paid them enough over the years to have earned a bit back. Let's hope the silly young bugger turns up.'

'It's solved one problem, anyway,' said Gauvinier, making a joke of it and not really succeeding. 'That's who I'm going to leave out of the team this afternoon. James and Paul aren't with us, which leaves eleven of us. Plus Oliver, of course. We'll have to share the scoring.'

In spite of the shadow over the tour, he felt their spirits rising as the coach rolled northwards up the valley of the Exe until it came to the hinterland where the Clysts are hidden from the gaze of all but the most persistent of tourists. Clyst St Cob was as idyllic a hamlet as Wym had been, but in its own thatched and whitewashed way. They passed between cottages that had been standing when Elizabeth I had reigned. There didn't seem space enough between the hills for a cricket pitch, but round the back of the Dun Horse, tucked in between the inn and the church, was a meadow of the purest green, sloping up to a wooden pavilion. No sign of a drought here, thought Gauvinier.

The cricket field was not flat – nothing could be really flat in this rolling country. From the lane which ran along beside the Dun Horse it rose quite substantially. The square was level enough, and the biggest dip was on the lane side, where the grass fell away under a line of mature chestnut trees, very similar to Tillingfold's own at home. Even the gnats busying themselves in the shade under the green leaves looked familiar. They parked in the little dusty car park behind the inn and ducked their way into the cool inside. A big man with grey curly hair closely lining a broad open face edged himself off his bar stool and came toward them, hand outstretched.

'Tillingfold?' You're earlier than we expected. Lunch is all ready. But you'll have a drink first, won't you. These are some of the guys.' He indicated a half a dozen men of varying ages. 'I'm hopeless at names.

Introduce yourselves. Which is your skipper?'

Gauvinier shook him by the hand.

'I'm Peter Gauvinier.'

'Graham, Graham Thoroughgood. Nice to see you. Have you had a good trip? Any luck?'

'Oh, we've had a great time. But we haven't won a game yet. Tied yesterday. With Trewartha,' he added proudly; for it was a good result to have run such a powerful club so close. The name Trewartha was known throughout the West Country.

'That's good going. But before you go any further, I must tell you what one of our Devon batsmen here did last season. Bob Merrifield, up at Clyst St George. He was playing in a Devon West league match. He hit two hundred and fifty-five in a hundred and seventy-seven minutes out of a total of three hundred and thirty for three declared. Thirty-nine fours and nineteen sixes. It isn't in the Guinness Book of Records yet, but it ought to be.'

Gauvinier whistled.

'I trust this Merrifield doesn't play for any other Clysts?'

'No. More's the pity. It sounds as if we could do with him against a side that tied with Trewartha.'

'Oh, I don't think you'll need anyone quite so formidable to deal with us. We're all a bit tired. And we've lost one of our better batsmen.' He explained about White, without mentioning the suspected theft or the breakfast tiff.

'He'll turn up,' said Thoroughgood cheerfully. 'It's the Devon air. It goes to your head. Or the clotted cream. Have you got enough people? D'you want a sub?'

Gauvinier shook his head.

'That's good. We've had a bit of a job to rake up a full team ourselves, this being a weekday. And our umpire can't make it.'

'We've brought our umpire, anyway, so that's one end taken care of. He's here.' He introduced Fanshawe.

Thoroughgood shook his hand. 'Glad you're here,' he said, looking closely at him. 'Fanshawe? *Fanshawe*? Weren't you with the 33rd Squadron? Ollie Fanshawe? You were my Wing-co. You were shot down. Jesus. We thought you were dead.'

'So did I. Several times,' said Fanshawe. 'I remember you, Thoroughgood. You went off the roof of the mess to try out your parachute and I grounded you for a week.'

'That's right, and Randy Mimms . . . Good God, this calls for a celebration. Ollie Fanshawe. You used to spend hours with those Wisdens of yours. Is he still a cricket buff?' Thoroughgood turned to Gauvinier. The fact that he had gone on himself to command his own wing and had just as many decorations for gallantry as Fanshawe did not seem to occur to him.

'Still a cricket buff,' said Gauvinier. 'More so than ever. We don't know what Tillingfold would do without him.'

Thoroughgood spotted Fanshawe's stick. It sobered him.

'Still in trouble, Ollie?'

Fanshawe nodded. He would never be out of trouble.

'It doesn't matter,' he said. 'I get by. But tell me. Whatever happened to . . .' and the two of them were away into a memory session; recalling the exploits of former comrades, many long dead and buried.

Gauvinier had not seen his friend so animated for years. He left them and joined the rest of the Tillingfold team, who had been making friends with the Clyst St Cob players. Or rather, the home side had been busily making friends with Gillian, whom they seemed to regard as a being from outer space.

'Is it true,' one demanded of Gauvinier, 'that this young lady of yours scored a fifty yesterday? Against Trewartha of all people?'

Gauvinier assured them it was perfectly true.

'Well, I never did.'

'Too right, George, you never did. Last time you scored a fifty the cow jumped over the moon.'

'If I ever scored a fifty the bloody cow would jump over the moon,' the young man replied, unabashed. 'Like the first time you take a wicket, young Harry.'

We'll see about that, George. I'll bet you a fiver I get a wicket before you get fifty.'

'You're on.' But, he explained to Tillingfold, the bet was unlikely ever to be paid out as he, George, was a bowler and batted regularly at number eleven; while Harry was an opening bat whose last remembered attempt at bowling was in an over-a-man beer match, in which he'd delivered six wides.

They all ate the pub's home-made steak and kidney pie for lunch, and felt better, if not as ready for cricket as they might, when they emerged blinking into the sunlight. Thoroughgood took Gauvinier out to toss up. He apologised for the wicket. 'It's not all that good, Peter. We keep promising ourselves we're going to re-lay it, but so far we haven't found the money. Something else always seems to crop up. Last year it was woodworm in the pavilion roof. Now it's new showers.'

'It looks all right to me. Heads!'

The coin came down. 'Heads it is. Your shout.'

Once again Gauvinier had no hesitation.

'We'll field. At least it'll give us time for the beer to go down.'

They strolled back to the pavilion in amity.

'What an astonishing coincidence, meeting Oliver,' said Thoroughgood. 'He was a bit of a god to us, you know. A fantastic pilot, as good as Bader, or anyone. He didn't have a nerve in him. I knew his fiancée, you know. Dorothy. A beautiful girl. It was a tragedy they never got married.'

'What happened to her?'

'Oh, she eventually got hitched to some naval type; a round the world yachtsman – Cunningham I think his name was. He was lost in the Atlantic in that freak storm about five years ago. She lives round here somewhere. I did hear she was a successful businesswoman.'

'Oliver's had a tough life.' said Gauvinier. 'Not much comfort in it for him. He can only do research work for the university, which doesn't bring in a great deal, and his pension doesn't go very far these days.'

'Humph.' Thoroughgood's snort condemned governments of every hue to damnation. They entered the pavilion, to find the subject of their conversation carefully polishing the new ball (provided by Bobby) on a yellow duster. He looked in no need of commiseration. He held up the ball for inspection.

'I think this will do, don't you?' Tossing it over.

Thoroughgood examined it with a critical air.

'Now I know why you like to bowl first. Clyst St Cob doesn't run to anything quite as classy. Pakistan for us. Much cheaper.'

'Oh, yes, and go out of shape in half an innings. Even in a village match,' said Fanshawe sternly. 'We found that by buying the more expensive balls, we were able to use them for the evening league knockabouts and the juniors as well, and still they'd be good enough for the nets. We saved a good £50 a season when we went back to English balls.'

Gauvinier chuckled. 'You're on to a Fanshawe hobby-horse,' he said.

'Not a bad one, either,' said Thoroughgood. 'But meeting Oliver has put right out of my mind what I meant to say. This young woman of yours seems to be quite a character. It's the first time I've ever heard of a girl playing with a men's team. How does it work?'

'Oh, we've had surprisingly little bother,' said Gauvinier. 'There was a bit of awkwardness at first in the dressing room, but Gill's a sensible girl and usually manages things so as not to embarrass the more sensitive among us. I've got a pretty strict rule about language – and a fines box – so that's helped. And as a player on the field she's done us proud time after time. You heard about yesterday.'

'Yes I did. Well, so long as we're not expected to take it easy on her.'

'She'd take it as an insult if you did. And hit you for four for your pains.'

'See you on the field.'

'Right.'

Before they could take to the field, however, a car drew up under the chestnuts, parked with its nose on the boundary, and disgorged three extremely pretty girls and, to their amazement, Paul White.

'Hullo Guv,' he said cheerfully. 'Sorry to have

missed the bus. Hullo Albert. Thanks for the loan of the jacket. 'You shouldn't leave things lying around, you know. You might lose something valuable.' He held out the jacket. 'Very comfortable,' he said. 'But the fit's not quite right. And I thought you'd be worried about your wallet. It's in the pocket. Thought I'd keep it safe for you.'

Jess, whose face was a picture, could not prevent himself from taking out the wallet and looking at its contents. They were still there, untouched, including the money.

'Don't you realise, you stupid young fool, that half the police in the county are looking for you?' he demanded. 'You could be inside the nick at any moment. And you'd bloody well deserve it.'

'But I'm not,' said Paul cockily 'Though I must admit that when that police car went by me up the road from the motel I did wonder.'

'What were you doing?'

'Hitching, of course. Lucky I had that jacket on. It made me look respectable.' He grinned at Jess.

'Respectable?' Jess choked down his anger. 'You have to laugh.' And laugh he did, and put out his hand.

'I'm glad you're back,' he said. 'Join the club.'

White was suddenly sheepish. 'Ta', he said. 'Sorry.' And sounded as if he meant it.

Gauvinier, a great weight lifted, said merely: 'We wondered where you'd got to. I'd be obliged if you'd take the scorebook.'

'Righto, Guv. My friends can help me.' They were very pretty girls indeed.

'Where,' said Trine, with some envy,' did you ever find a trio like that?'

Ah,' Paul tapped the side of his nose. 'Ask no

questions and you'll hear no lies. Actually, they're from America, or Canada or somewhere. Their idea of roughing it is to hire a limo, as they call it, and pick up handsome young fellers like me hitching a lift to cricket matches. And when they heard this was where I was going, Mavis – that's the redhead – said: "Gee, a village cricket match. Say, that would be darling."' Paul managed a fair imitation of a Californian drawl. 'And they've got loot,' he added.

Gauvinier laughed. Trust young White to land with his bum in the butter.

'Go on, then, keep the scorebook. But don't mess it up. Bobby would never forgive you.'

The players were divided in their attitudes to the return of the prodigal.

'Should chuck him out of the club,' muttered Deacon under his breath, but so he could be heard.

'Deserves a bloody good hiding,' was Hunter's verdict.

'Stupid young bugger,' said Trine. 'But what a comeback.' He whistled.

'Beauties and the beast, eh?' said Jess. 'If that young man fell in a midden, he'd come up smelling of lavender water.'

'Just what I was thinking, only more elegantly put,' said Gauvinier. Then, more sharply, 'That's enough. Paul's back and that's that. He'll be scoring this afternoon.'

That was all that was said, although Paul summoned up a wave to Gillian as the team went into the field.

'Sorry, Gilly,' he called, and Gillian waved back. 'No bones broken,' she said.

'There might have been,' said Jess. 'But the young fool had the sense not to struggle.' And they took their places in the field.

Whether it was a sort of end of term feeling, or because it was the last match of a strenuous four days' tour, Tillingfold voted afterwards that the Clyst St Cob match was the most enjoyable of them all. There was the relief that White had returned, without trouble, and a double relief, for scores of aching bones and muscles, that this was the last game of the tour. 'At least,' Trine said afterwards, 'We got some idea of what the professionals go through.' So Norman Smith ran up to bowl with just a little more bounce to his step, and the fielders closed in on the batsman with that little extra tautness to their bearing which always gave Gauvinier a thrill.

'At least James isn't here to hold things back,' he thought, and then chided himself for being uncharitable. But his thought was compounded when Gillian, fielding 'round the corner' instead of at gully, where Fred Bason stood on massive guard, swooped to her left and neatly picked off an elegant leg-glance from the Clyst batsman, who happened to be Harry, who had made the bet in the bar.

'Why is there only one girl on the field?' Mavis asked Paul, the first of a stream of questions which played havoc with his attention to his scoring. 'And why don't they have numbers on their backs, so we can see who's who? They all look the same in their little white pants.'

'She's the only girl because this is really a man's game. But she's a bloody good player,' said White, surprised to find himself championing Gillian. 'Did you see that stop?'

But the finer points of the game had not yet been ingested by Mavis.

'You sweet on her?' she asked, and laughed to

see him blush.

'No, of course not. It's just that . . .' he found himself tongue-tied.

'It's just what?' she probed.

'Oh, I don't know. But she's doing something plenty of other girls could do, I reckon, if they wanted to. They just haven't got the guts. A cricket ball,' he added severely, 'is very hard. Women are usually too soft for it.' And to emphasise his point, a neatly-driven four cracked against the wooden paling in front of his scorer's table and rebounded into the field of play. The girls, who had recoiled from the impact, looked impressed.

'But she doesn't look tough,' objected Mavis, who seemed to be the spokesman for the three of them. 'Oh-oh, she goofed.'

Gillian had failed to hold a stiff chance pulled round the corner by the second Clyst opening batsman. She chased after the ball and returned it to Deacon to some sympathetic applause, while the batsmen made a comfortable two runs.

Mavis lost interest in Gillian.

'Why's that man – the one with the ball now? What's wrong with him?'

White explained about Budgeon's polio.

'Gee, that's wonderful,' Mavis breathed. 'You wouldn't get a cripple playing baseball like that.'

'Watch out,' White interrupted her. The ball had been hit hard again in their direction, bouncing twice before crashing into the pavilion wall behind them. Mavis picked it up. 'Gee. It is hard too. What'll I do with it?'

'Just chuck it to me,' said Trine, the fielder, who had given up the unequal chase. 'I say, Paul. I like your helpers.' And he grinned amiably at all three girls. 'See you later,' he said indiscriminately. He rather hoped Quincey Wym would not turn up.

'Who's that?'

'Oh, that's Trine. Teddy Trine. Our local lord of the manor's son. Playing with the people, see.'

'And who's that one. The grey-haired man?'

'That's Gauvinier, the captain. His dad was captain before him. He's an advertising man.' And before he knew it White was running through the team.

'Norman, that's the bowler at the other end, he works in a stables. He's just been made head groom. Fred Bason, the fat one at gully next to Guv – that's the skipper – he's a builder. The chap next to him runs the local garage. He's Frank Hunter, who drove our coach down. We call them Frank'n'Fred in the village. They're always at each other. Bill Budgeon, he's the cobbler. And that big bloke at mid-off' – he pointed – 'he's the Reverend Veysey, the parson. Good bat, too. And that one out there' – he pointed to the far side of the field – 'at cover point, you'll have heard of him. He's Jess, Albert Jess. The pop star.'

'Oh,' said Mavis, vaguely interested. 'Yes, I remember. He used to top the charts a few years ago.' She dismissed Jess and concentrated her attention on the present. 'And what do you do?'

'Nothing very much,' said White. 'I read meters. Electricity meters.'

'Why aren't you playing today?'

'Well, that's a long story,' said White. 'And I'm not telling you. But someone's got to stand down. There are only eleven in the team, and there are thirteen of us on the tour.'

Mavis contemplated the sunlit field, the whites of the

players and the shade of the chestnuts.

'Gee,' she said softly, 'I like cricket. It's all moving patterns. I haven't got the helluvan idea what's going on, but it looks like a painting. Like it was centuries old.' She yawned. 'But it's a bit slow.'

'You wait,' said White. 'You wait until the end. It often gets exciting then.'

'How long's that?'

White looked at the church clock. 'Oh, about four hours from now.'

'I can't wait,' she said. 'I want my excitement now. Come on, girls. Let's go. See ya maybe.' She waved an elegant hand and ushered her companions into the car. White watched them go, with regret. He thought he knew what 'excitement now' meant. He had no hope of ever seeing them again.

'What have you done with them?' said Trine from the boundary.

'They took one look at you, Teddy boy, and ran a mile. They'll be back,' he said with false confidence.

'Good,' said Trine. 'I don't think Quim's coming today, after all.'

Whatever hatchet had appeared at breakfast time seemed to be buried.

'You get on with the game,' said White, and turned his attention to the scorebook, checking and cross-checking quickly to see that he'd made no errors. Not all that much had happened, so far. Clyst St Cob had progressed to twenty-eight for the loss of no wickets. Harry Grouse, the opening batsman had made twenty of these, and his partner, Golightly, had made eight. There were no byes, leg-byes or no-balls to cope with. Not very exciting, as Mavis had said. But Mavis had left too early. Excitement was about to begin.

Harry Grouse called for a new bat. There didn't seem much wrong with the old one, but Tillingfold learned later that Grouse made a fetish of calling for a new bat when he felt he had not got his eye in. It was time Clyst St Cob moved into another gear. Thoroughgood, who had donned the Clyst umpire's white coat for the first few overs, said aside to Gillian, who was fielding near him: 'You'll see something now.'

Actually, Grouse did something with which few batsmen would agree. He changed his bat for one about four ounces heavier. Normally a batsman who can afford to run to two bats tries to choose them at nearly exactly the same weight and balance, so that, should a change become necessary during an innings, it does not affect the timing and that all-important 'feel'. Years ago, Grouse had broken a bat after scoring twenty or so, and gone on to make a century with the only spare bat left in the club bag – a monstrous old Gunn and Moore which had survived only as it was too heavy for the rest of the team. Since that innings he had made a shibboleth of it, as many batsmen do of all sorts of things, changing his bat religiously every time he happened to get into the twenties.

However, today was not one of Harry's better ones. There was excitement all right. Harry signalled the arrival of his heavier bat by advancing two paces up the wicket before Norman Smith had even reached the crease. Whap! The ball crashed through the covers to the boundary. The next ball Grouse swung with flat-batted fury past Trine at long on; and when Norman bowled his next ball two feet wide of the off stump and as fast as he could, Joe Deacon made a splendid stumping with Grouse stranded in mid-stream, as it were. Swinging his heavy bat cheerfully, he strode back to the pavilion, having at least woken up a quiet Friday afternoon for a sleepy village.

Norman trotted down the wicket to share congratulations with Deacon.

'I saw you coming, Joe,' he said.

'I dare say you did,' said Deacon, who had crept up close to the wicket while Grouse had been occupied with advancing on Norman. 'But there was no call to have bowled so wide. Put two feet on my arms, it did, to reach it. I'm surprised the umpire didn't call wide.'

But he was too pleased with the stumping to continue. Swinging his arms wide, out and back, he mimed the stumping action through again.

'If it was as wide as that,' said Bason behind him, 'you'll go down in the Guinness Book of Records, Joe.'

'I wouldn't be surprised then, Fred.' The little wicketkeeper nodded his head vigorously. 'T'was a long way outside the off stump, you know.'

'That's all right, Joe,' said Budgeon, who had been standing at slip. 'If you'd missed I'd have taken it down the leg side.' But the gentle irony went over Joe's head.

'That's all very well,' he said. 'But you won't find many keepers stumping from as far out as that.'

'Ay, nor many as'll make so much shout about it,' said Bason.

Gauvinier's 'Man in!' called them to order, and Budgeon, who was told that this over would be his last unless he had a bit of luck, produced two nearly perfect deliveries to take two wickets in the space of four balls. The first removed the second Clyst opener, Golightly, moving away from him as the bat came through in an apparently firm defensive stroke, the ball careering fast and low off the edge to Bason's right where a massive red hand seized it safely. There was no tumbling; no heroics. At one moment the ball was flashing through the air; the next it was couched in Bason's hand, and the unfortunate batsman was still looking towards the third man boundary when the umpire's finger was raised in response to Bason's quietly confident 'How was that, Mr Umpire?'

His successor, a left-handed batsman of great freedom of whom the Clyst captain had told Gauvinier much was expected, lasted three balls. How the first missed the wicket no-one knew; how Deacon missed it as it passed by his pads on its way to four byes most of Tillingfold told him afterwards. He threw up his hands in a gigantic appeal as the ball swung past the leg stump, eluding his half-instinctive movement to race its way to the boundary.

The second ball had the batsman 'going every which way' as Budgeon said later. He shuffled across his wicket with his right, front foot, bringing the bat across in front of his pads and clipping the ball off the toe of his bat onto his own big toe. Budgeon stifled an appeal and wondered how he could further bewilder the unfortunate man. He had that rare feeling of power that comes over a bowler when he is right on top of a batsman. He switched his grip on the ball to one across the seam, not along it and, rolling his wrist, delivered the fiercest leg-break spin his powerful wrist and fingers could conjure up. As it curled away from his hand he saw it swing away in the air to the left-hander's off side. The batsman's right foot went across, the bat poised to drive. Suddenly the ball seemed to dip and broke fiercely from a foot outside the batsman's off stump, beating the bat and cannoning off his pads into the wicket. The batsman stared in disbelief at his wrecked stumps. 'Strewth!' he said.

'Ay,' said Deacon. 'And if it hadn't hit your pads it'd have gone for four past square leg. It turned a bloody yard if it turned an inch.'

Budgeon beamed. He was not normally a spin bowler. And he could have told nobody what imp of inspiration led him to change grip, style and everything about his delivery with such certainty.

'Well bowled, Bill,' Gauvinier said, pumping him by the hand. He was always delighted with Budgeon's successes. 'Where on earth did you produce that one from?'

'Ah,' said Budgeon with perfect honesty. 'That came from the back of my hand, that did. He didn't have much idea, did he?' He grinned in delight.

There was no stopping him now. In his next over he produced a near-perfect top-spinner which leapt through Graham Thoroughgood's defence and took the top of the middle stump; and then took his fourth wicket with what appeared to be a slow, gentle yorker, but which Deacon swore swung both ways in the air before bowling the Clyst wicketkeeper neck and crop.

'Now what the devil did you do to that one?' Gauvinier didn't really care, but it did appear that Budgeon was possessed of a most welcome demon.

'Don't you listen to Joe, Guv,' said Budgeon. 'That bloke got himself out. T'were nothing but a good straight ball. That's all. Didn't break nor swing more'n a hairsbreadth. It's this wicket. T'was born for me, or I for it.'

With five wickets down and the score not yet forty, Gauvinier was in a dilemma that most captains would have welcomed. It appeared he had only to keep his two bowlers on and the Clyst side would collapse like a pack of cards. On the other hand, this made it look likely that the match would be all over by teatime, and although a comfortable win would look good when the reports of the tour were published in the *County Times*, Gauvinier didn't like easy wins, and hated 'beer matches', those fill-in games in which every person bowled an over and the losers paid for the beer. Gauvinier, who liked to win, also liked to win a good fight, and he was pondering the equation when the matter was rather taken out of his hands. Or rather put into the hands of a vast, red-bearded figure who strode to the wicket wearing one pad and no batting gloves, and carrying the oldest, darkest piece of willow any of them had ever seen. It looked like mercantile teak, and Gauvinier felt, probably weighed as much. In the giant's hands it looked like a matchstick.

'Bloody hell. W.G. himself,' Trine muttered under his breath promising to pass on the thought to Jess at the over's end. The giant took guard with meticulous care, bumped his bat in the block a couple of times, then strode in a full circle round the wicket, fixing each fieldsman in turn with a piercing blue stare. Then he hit Smith's ball onto the roof of the Dun Horse, sending a tile clattering from the roof.

'W.G. indeed,' thought Trine grimly, as he found a gap in the garden fence and retrieved the ball.

Norman Smith didn't like being hit for six, and his next ball reared wickedly from just short of a length and rapped the huge batsman under the beard.

'Are you all right?' Gauvinier inquired anxiously as he trotted forward to pick up the ball. The giant rubbed his ribs a couple of times. 'No harm,' he said, swatting with his bat an an imaginary wasp. And he swatted the next ball from Norman onto the roof of the Dun Horse again, bringing another tile clattering down and sending Trine on another hunt through the vegetable garden. A small rotund figure emerged from the Dun Horse, looked up at the damage and across the pitch to the batsman causing it and shrugged its shoulders with resignation. 'Oh, Brewster,' it said, and went back inside.

Norman put his heart into producing his best bowling, and drew from the giant two perfectly respectable and respectful defensive strokes, weight well forward on the front foot. Off the last ball of the over, Brewster shaped to put the ball over the Dun Horse again, changed his mind and flicked a little cut down to third man, walking the single and flatly refusing his partner's urging to make it two.

He hit Budgeon's first ball fearfully hard a foot off the ground but straight at the bowler. Budgeon couldn't have got out of the way had he wanted to. He put down two hands in automatic reaction to try for the catch. It was like trying to catch a cannon ball. It crashed through his spread fingers and thumped into his knee with a sound like a whipcrack. Budgeon went down as though shot, clutching his leg and rolling over in agony. Gauvinier, not caring what had happened to the ball, raced up the pitch to the stricken bowler, who was holding his right knee with both hands and moaning gently. As he bent down, Gauvinier found himself shouldered aside by a soft but irresistible force, as the big batsman, his face contorted with anxiety, knelt down beside Budgeon.

'Christ, lad I'm sorry. Christ, I'm sorry,' he whispered. 'I wouldn't have hurt you for the world. Let me see, laddie. Let me see.' And his huge fingers fell over the bruised kneee as Budgeon tried to sit up.

'I'll be all right,' he said in a strangled voice.

'Nothing broken, I think. But you'd better go to the doctor.'

Budgeon took Brewster's arm and helped himself to his feet, but when he tried to stand the knee collapsed again, and he sagged against the big batsman.

'You can't walk on that just yet.'

Brewster put down his bat and, picking up Budgeon as though he were a child, carried him towards the pavilion, followed by a distressed clutch of Tillingfold players.

Thoroughgood leapt into action, using his officer's voice.

'Harry, get your car. George, you go with them and take him down to casualty at the county hospital. Get them to X-ray that knee. And put a blanket over him. We don't want him to die of shock.'

Budgeon opened both eyes. His face was pale with pain.

'It'll take more than a bloody cricket ball to kill me. I'm all right,' he said. 'Let me down, mate. I can stand.'

And stand he did, despite the pain. 'There's nothing broke,' he said. 'I'll be walking in a minute. Let me take a couple of overs off, Guv, and I'll be back as good as new.'

Thoroughgood said anxiously, 'Are you sure you're OK? Come on, let's run you down for a check-up. That was a hell of a belt.'

Budgeon looked down at his twisted legs. He grinned wryly.

'Reckon I can put up with a bit of pain, at that,' he said. 'Don't you worry about me. I'm all right.' His Sussex accent was very broad. 'I'll just sit here and rub the bugger.' Which he proceeded to do, vigorously, while the players returned slowly to their game.

Gauvinier took the ball to complete Budgeon's over. However compassionate the bearded giant may have seemed to a stricken foe, it obviously did not extend to his colleagues who were still upright, and he hit Gauvinier for two fours and a six off his five balls. Fortunately, Brewster could not bat at both ends at the same time, and Norman was allowed an over in which to put his length and direction together again, and then Gauvinier had another go. It was the bludgeon against the rapier, and the bludgeon won, hands down. Gauvinier's subtle shifts of line and length were treated with cavalier contempt, the ball rattling the boundary fences four times and clearing them once.

'Norman,' said Gauvinier at the end of the over. 'You try to keep this end quiet and we'll ring the changes at the other end. I'll try Frank first.'

Frank did his best. He produced one beautiful googly which clattered off the roof of the pavilion, three bad balls which the batsman unaccountably missed, and two good length orthodox leg breaks which were driven into the sightscreen just beyond the leaping Trine's upstretched hands.

'Your turn, Fred.'

Bason's off-breaks were treated similarly, except that twenty came that over in place of eighteen and with some reluctance Gauvinier turned to Gillian. 'Have a go, Jill, and let's see what he can do to you.'

He could, and did quite a lot. Gauvinier placed every Tillingfold fielder on the boundary except for a slip, and gave Gillian no more instruction than to bowl a length. Brewster hit her for five fours and a single, finding the gaps in the field by sheer weight of shot rather than by any form of placing.

'Bloody hell,' said Jess. We're being crucified.'

At that moment, there was a flutter from the pavilion. 'Skipper, Skipper.'

Gauvinier ran over, worried that Budgeon's knee had collapsed completely. It was Paul White.

'Look, Guv,' he said. 'Bill here reckons he's all right to carry on. But I can field, if you can persuade the silly bugger to stay here and nurse his knee for a bit.'

'Go on, Bill.' Gauvinier was more than usually authoritative. 'Do what he says. Paul can field for us as twelfth man.' He asked Thoroughgood, who assented cheerfully, though not without the warning: 'But he can't bat for you as well.' It saved him sending a substitute fielder out.

Budgeon took over the scorebook while White dragged on his flannels and ran onto the field, still wearing his training shoes. Tillingfold greeted him with modified applause, some, from Jess and Trine, slightly ironic. Gauvinier waved him to cover point and adjusted the field.

Now Norman was bowling to the fearful Brewster. The ball was short, rising off the uneven pitch. The batsman swung, hard and high off the top edge of the bat. Paul, racing round from cover point, his arms outstretched, sensed Jess converging on him from third man and checked, just in time. Jess, at full tilt, made contact with the ball with both hands as he stumbled forward and fell, losing it along the ground. The batsman, watching the fielder and not the ball in the middle of his run, hesitated as White grabbed the ball as it trickled towards the boundary and launched it, flat and hard, at the bowler's wicket. Fast and sure, the ball sped over fifty yards, hitting the wicket full-pitch as Brewster lunged for the crease, beating his bat by a yard and a half.

'Not out,' said the Clyst umpire, who by now was Golightly, the opening batsman. Brewster looked at him in disbelief.

'What's the matter with you, laddie?' he inquired. 'Blind? Deaf? Dumb? I was out by a bloody yard.' And marched off with his bat held high, acknowledging the whole-hearted cheers of the players of both sides.

The scoreboard was transformed in under half an hour's play. A miserable forty for five wickets was transformed to a hundred and twenty-five for six, of which the giant blacksmith had made seventy-seven.

Back at the pavilion, Brewster made straight for Budgeon, who was scoring and sitting awkwardly, still rubbing his knee. 'Still hurting, mate?' he asked. 'I'm bloody sorry to have caught you one like that.'

'T'was all my fault,' said Budgeon. 'I shoulda caught the bugger. Got both hands to it, too. But you do hit bloody hard. What do you do? Blacksmith?'

'Blacksmith, thatcher, hedger. You name it. I do it. Come on. Let's have a look at your knee.'

Budgeon hitched up his trouser leg, exposing his knee. The leg was twisted out of shape, the knee bulging large. He was embarrassed.

'It's always like that,' he said. 'Don't worry about it.'

The ball had missed the kneecap, but a dark bruise was beginning to spread lividly in the muscle immediately above it. Brewster prodded it with surprisingly sensitive fingers. 'I'll get you summat for that,' he said. 'It's just over at the smithy.'

He strode off, pad still strapped on his leg, and within two minutes was back with a large piece of flannel, a bottle of some yellow-green mixture, and a bandage. He folded the flannel carefully, and dosed it liberally with the yellow liquid. A pungent smell floated round the chestnuts.

'Liniment,' said Brewster briefly. 'It'll warm you up a bit. Does the horses no end of good.' He bound the bandage round the bruised leg. Instantly Budgeon felt a warm glow soothing the bruised muscle.

'Eeh, that feels a sight better already. Thanks.' He stood up gingerly and put his weight on the leg. 'Yes, I can stand up now. I'll be getting back on the field.'

'You just sit down and let the stuff work,' said Brewster. 'That young bloke who took your place is doing all right. He ran me out a treat. Wonder what that stupid Golightly was thinking about? I was out by over a yard. How d'you manage to play with legs like that?' He looked down at his own massive thighs, strong as tree trunks.

'It's no bother. You get used to it.'

'I think it's bloody marvellous. You were bowling like a bomb before I clobbered you.'

'Ah, it's the wicket. That one was made for me. You get a wicket like that and you can make it talk. Hadn't been for you, we'd have had you all out by now.'

Brewster looked out to see what was happening.

'Actually, you have.'

The last four batsmen had succumbed tamely, Norman and Gillian sharing their wickets – a catch and another good stumping by Deacon, who was beside himself with pleasure. Two stumpings and a catch behind was more than his usual ration.

Budgeon was the centre of concern, but he quickly put their minds at ease.

'Don't fuss. It'll be all right to bat. The blacksmith here has dosed me up with some horse liniment and its getting better by the moment.'

'Horse liniment?' Norman Smith worked with

horses. 'That'll take your skin off.'

'Not mine,' said Brewster. 'It's my own recipe. I got it from my old father. 'This'll fix man and beast,' he used to tell me. And it does.'

'That's right enough,' said Thoroughgood. 'Joe Brewster used to doctor men and horses round here for years. I reckon young Jack has inherited the old skills.'

'Well,' said Norman. 'I could do with some of that stuff myself for my horses. I could even drink a gallon of it.'

There was a chorus of assent. It had been hot and dusty fielding. They trooped out with one accord to the white-clothed tables laid under the chestnut trees, with two great urns at the head of each table, and man-sized mugs ready for the filling.

Plates of sandwiches, ham, cheese and cucumber, were decorated with ripe tomatoes, and large wedges of fruit-cake stood ready for the taking. Tillingfold, who were accustomed to a very good tea at home, were impressed, and in spite of their weariness, piled in manfully.

'Sorry there's no jam, said a Clyst man. 'It brings out the wasps.'

'A hundred and thirty five,' said Gauvinier to Jess. 'It might take some getting, on this pitch.'

'A hundred and thirty five,' Jess repeated. 'It's a doddle.' And he took a huge swig of tea and collapsed, choking, as it 'went down the wrong way' as he said when Gauvinier had thumped him mightily on the back.

Chapter Eight

IT WAS NO DODDLE.

Jess and Gauvinier himself went out to open the response to Clyst St Cob's total of a hundred and thirty-four at precisely 5.30. By six o'clock Gauvinier had scored exactly eleven runs while watching four wickets fall at the other end, all to a tall, curly-haired man of about thirty who looked just what Jess had said – a doddle.

His name was Larkin, and Gauvinier had noticed when he went out to bat briefly at the end of the Clyst innings that he was a cricketer of large enthusiasm. His forward defensive prod was made with exaggerated care, the foot plonking down heavily beside the carefully-sloped bat. When he hooked a ball from Gillian for four, the bat came through with a flourish, and he followed the flight of the ball with a seraphic smile on his face. Now, as a bowler, Larkin was – or should have been – a doddle.

He took a short run, holding the ball in both hands in front of his face. At the bowling stride, a large foot plunged forward and thumped on the ground, well within the popping crease. The right arm went back, straight, and looped over again, straight, as the ball was dispatched in a gentle parabola high into the sky. So high, in fact, that it tended to clear the top of the rather small sightscreen and lose itself, so far as the batsman was concerned, in the dappled leaves of the chestnut background.

'Even so,' said Jess, discussing the phenomenon afterwards, 'When the ball came down it was still so gentle that you had all the time in the world to hit it into the middle of next week.'

Jess hit it straight back into the middle of Larkin's stomach, where two large hands pouched it safely and gratefully, and the seraphic smile, which Gauvinier had seen before, reappeared.

That was one wicket down for no runs.

At the other end, Gauvinier faced his opposing skipper, Thoroughgood, who bowled a brisk medium pace and kept the ball at an awkward length for scoring. Gauvinier managed a two from a rather thick-edged drive past point.

Tillingfold's number three batsman was today the Reverend Richard Veysey, generally restored to health and recruited back into the side by necessity, once Mitterman was away and young White had gone walkabout. He took a careful guard and watched the looping ball with interest.

The first three balls he patted gravely back up the wicket to the bowler. The fourth he moved down the wicket to nicely and drove spendidly through the covers for four runs. He tried to repeat the shot off the fifth ball, but somehow found it dropping short of his forward plunge. He checked himself just in time and blocked it. To the sixth he played forward with extreme care, watching bemused as the ball bounced gently 'through the gate' (the gap between bat and pad) and just as gently removed his leg bail.

That was two wickets down for six runs.

Gauvinier coped with Thoroughgood again, hitting a nice drive for two and another, moving his feet in that unconsciously balletic movement known to all real cricketers, through mid-wicket for four. But Thoroughgood pinned him back in defence off the last two balls, and he did not manage to get the single he wanted; and so Bobby Bewers, the new batsman, was left to face Larkin, who was beginning to assume the stature of an ogre in Tillingfold minds.

Bewers didn't mind. He would prefer, he thought, to face a nice slow toss-up bowler like Larkin than a pace man any day. At sixteen he had not yet found that confidence that would enable him to enjoy batting against fast bowling. This dolly-dropping stuff was for him.

He finished the over still at the wicket, which on reflection was quite a feat. For the dolly-dropping bowler had tied his young victim into so many knots that he almost began to wish he'd still been sitting with the score book.

As he missed the sixth ball, scrambling his right foot back into the crease just in time to avoid being stumped by Brewster, standing massively behind the wicket, Bobby dropped his bat, scratched his head with both gloved hands and shook it sadly. Gauvinier came down the pitch.

'Just take it steady, Bobby. I'll try to get up this end to take the blighter. He's pretty deceptive. Just play a straight bat and keep your eye on the ball.'

'That's what I'm trying to do, Guv. But I can't seem to fathom him at all.'

'Good luck.' And Gauvinier managed to hit a three off the first ball of Thoroughgood's next over to take him to the other end, where he watched with some satisfaction as Bewers coped manfully with the more orthodox bowling of the Clyst skipper. But the lad snicked the last ball down the leg side, and Gauvinier was forced to take a single. He still had not faced Larkin's bowling.

The curly-haired bowler smiled his gentle smile at Bobby and lobbed the ball higher than ever. Bobby tried hard to follow his captain's advice and play a straight bat, but at the last moment he thought he had another answer. He leapt out, whirled his bat and missed the ball completely. The wicketkeeper removed the bails softly, almost apologetically.

'Sorry, son. You're out,' he said in his gentle voice.

That was three wickets down for twelve runs.

Gauvinier wished he could have spared young Trine the humiliation. Trine, who believed all slow bowlers had been heaven-sent for his flashing blade, stepped lightly to the wicket with a smile on his face, which said, 'I'm going to fix this blighter.' He advanced down the wicket to his first ball, took a mighty swing, missed completely, overbalanced and was stumped lying in the centre of the pitch two yards out of his crease. He took himself back to the pavilion, bemused.

That was four wickets down for twelve runs, of which Gauvinier had scored eleven. But he still had not faced Larkin.

At least, he thought, Fred Bason would not succumb to similar rushes of the blood. Fred could be relied upon to plant his broad body behind his broad bat and meet every challenge head down. Things were becoming a matter of survival now for Tillingfold; winning had faded from the agenda.

Fred Bason took his slow guard, studied the bowler carefully, and seemingly unmindful of the crisis, played the next four balls calmly back down the wicket. The ball made a series of reassuring thuds on the middle of his bat. He made no attempt to score runs. At the end of the over, he walked sturdily up to Gauvinier.

'I think I've got this bloke sussed,' he said. 'You get the runs, Guv. I'll keep my end up.'

And keep his end up he did, for a full forty-five minutes, scoring only two runs in all that time while Gauvinier, his mind relieved by the sight of such broad confidence, prospered at the other end. The battle between Bason and Larkin became something of an epic. The bowler tossed the ball up, higher and higher. The batsman met it with his stolid forward prod, the bat seemingly growing broader as the afternoon wore on. It seemed there would be no end to the stalemate. After an hour, Tillingfold had scored fifty-one runs, of which Gauvinier had made forty-six. Bason had two, and there were three no-balls, all from George Green, who had relieved Thoroughgood as Gauvinier's confidence grew.

In all this time, Gauvinier had still not played a ball from Larkin. Now he forced Bason into a fiercely run single at the end of a Green over, and took guard for the first time against the looping menace. He had had a long time to study the bowler from the non-striker's end, and he had come to the conclusion that the deception was all in the flight. There was little turn when the ball met the pitch; every ball appeared to be hittable. Gauvinier, back on his stumps, played the first three balls with due respect. When the third came he made a little room for himself and cut it hard, accurately bisecting the gap between cover point and gully. A cheer from the pavilion announced his side's relief, and his own fifty.

Determined not to be drawn out of his crease, Gauvinier played the next ball defensively; he put his right foot well across the wicket to the last and pulled it as hard as he could towards the mid-wicket boundary. Perhaps the ball bounced slightly high, or more slowly than he expected; instead of clearing mid-wicket easily, the ball sailed well within catching distance of the unfortunate Golightly, whose flustered attempt at a catch left him sucking his fingers and cursing gently to himself. Gauvinier accepted two runs with thanks. He would not make the same mistake again.

There was less than an hour left now for play, and some time ago Fanshawe had looked at his watch and called 'last twenty' to the scorer's table, where Paul White had re-established himself. Now there were sixteen overs left, and Tillingfold needed seventy-five to win. To win? Hearts lifted in the pavilion as the visitors realised that the game could still be won.

'Good old Guv. Watch him go.'

'Play up, play up, Tillingfold.' The old cry of support that had been handed down the years floated from the pavilion. Gauvinier recognised it with a brief catch at the throat. He felt excited, lifted by their confidence, which was almost tangible. But nearly five runs an over was a stiff task. And Fred was no hitter.

Suddenly, Fred was no more. Perhaps relieved by getting away from Larkin, his tormentor, he swung uncharacteristically at Green and was bowled.

That was sixty for five wickets; Gauvinier fifty-four. Four more than his age. The incongruous thought distracted him for a moment. Oh well, let's double that. There was nothing he couldn't do. With Frank Hunter now nearly a sleeping partner at the other end, Gauvinier charged into the attack. He drove arrogantly, cut without mercy, flicked and glanced at will. The menace of Larkin was dismissed from memory in two overs of uninhibited attack. Tillingfold raced past the century. And then with eighty-five under his belt, Gauvinier hooked once more at a Larkin dolly-drop; once more the bounce was deceptive. It was the same mistake as before, the one he had sworn not to repeat. And this time Golightly clutched the catch and held on to it thankfully, despite his injured fingers. Gauvinier hardly heard Gillian's 'Well batted, Guv' as she passed him on the way to the wicket. He was clapped off the field by the Clyst team, and into the pavilion by his own; but Gauvinier heard nothing. He was consumed by disappointment; he had seen Tillingfold to the verge of victory, and then let them down.

'Marvellous knock, skip. Bloody marvellous.'

'Never seen a better one.'

'Well done, Peter. Well done indeed.'

The congratulations poured over him as he removed his pads wearily from his sweaty legs, threw his box into his bag and, draping a sweater round his shoulders, went out to watch the finish of the game. He felt drained; and yet elation was beginning to return. After all, eighty-five out of a total of a hundred and two was not bad. Not bad at all. For a man of fifty.

Thirty-three to win. Gillian at the wicket, already the heroine of one tight finish. Six overs to go. Frank Hunter, taking over the leading role now his captain was out, pulling a four to the long on boundary, past Golightly. Cheers from the pavilion. He tried again, and this time a shout from behind signified a catch. The keeper had dived, incredibly, three yards to his left to take an astonishing ball, one-handed and so close to the ground that Frank looked twice at the man on the ground and back to the umpire's finger before walking.

'Good catch,' he said doubtfully, and the keeper, who knew he had taken the ball cleanly, grinned up at him from the ground with pleasure. 'Bloody lucky,' he said.

Twenty-nine runs to win. Five overs left. Three wickets to fall; and one of those to an injured cripple.

'Are you really fit to bat? Gauvinier asked Budgeon who, with no great faith in those who were to precede him, was already buckling on a pad.

'You just stop me, Guv,' Budgeon grinned at him. 'Anyway, I probably won't be needed.'

A shout from outside gave him the lie. Norman, forgetting his seasons of coaching at Gauvinier's hands, had tried to hit Larkin out of the ground, just as Trine had, and suffered much the same fate. However, not before he had collected eight runs from two mighty swipes.

Twenty-one runs to win; four overs left.

Deacon joined Gillian, who had not yet scored. Thoroughgood brought himself back on to bowl, to make the final breakthrough. He could keep Larkin going the other end, now the recognised batsmen had all gone. Deacon, backing away as usual from the faster bowler, offered a simple catch into the gully.

Twenty runs to win. Three overs left. The last pair in. Budgeon, limping even more heavily than usual, greeted Gillian.

'We've done this before,' he grinned. 'Don't let's muck it up this time.'

Gillian faced Larkin, every nerve extended. She watched the ball like a hawk. It floated high, but this time too far, and she pulled the full toss firmly round to the long-leg boundary. 'That's right, lass,' called Budgeon. 'Let's get 'em in fours.' She knew he wasn't joking, and tried to hit another boundary in the same spot. Budgeon limped the single and, without bothering to take guard, hit Larkin a tremendous blow to cover point. Four more runs.

Eleven runs to win now, with two overs to go. Thoroughgood bowling to Gillian. 'No damned girl is going to beat us,' he muttered to himself, hurling down his fastest inswinger. She met it firm as a rock, the blade straight, head over the ball, the shot timed beautifully. Like an arrow the ball pierced the leg field.

Seven to win. And Gillian cut Thoroughgood once more to the boundary in that over, leaving Budgeon to thrash the winning runs off Larkin with another scything sweep. Tillingfold had won, in the last over, by one wicket and with five balls to spare. Larkin had taken seven wickets for twenty-nine runs.

In the excitement of the closing overs Gauvinier had not noticed a low black BMW which had driven up quietly and parked itself under the chestnut trees. The finish had drawn a few villagers carrying pints of dark beer from the Dun Horse, mingling with the players in the flurry of congratulations.

'What a game!' Thoroughgood shook him warmly by the hand. 'What an innings, skip. Pity you didn't get your ton. You deserved it.'

'Yes, great knock.' Larkin, the curly-haired bowler, already had a pint in his hand.

'Well, that was a great piece of bowling. You must give our slow men some advice.'

'I just toss it up into the trees, and if the sun's there that's even better.' Larkin smiled his seraphic smile. 'It doesn't often come off as well as today, though. Usually I get belted all round the park.'

'You fair mesmerised us,' said Gauvinier, his attention distracted by a figure waving to him from the parked car. It extracted itself from the car and came slowly across the grass, turning into James Mitterman. Gauvinier greeted him with enthusiasm.

'Did you see the finish, James? Weren't they great – Little Gill and Bill? No trouble. Whack, and they did it.' Mitterman smiled at his enthusiasm.

'I'm told you didn't do so badly yourself, Peter. I've had a good day, too. If you've a moment, I'd like you to meet my new business partner.' He guided Gauvinier over to the BMW. An elegant woman of indeterminate age was seated behind the driving wheel.

'Peter Gauvinier, this is Mrs Cunningham. Our captain, Peter. We've signed a deal today which I think is going to suit us both.' Mitterman beamed expansively. Mrs Cunningham smiled graciously and shook Gauvinier's fingers with a fawn gloved hand. He could see that she was dressed all in fawn, with an amber brooch holding a silk scarf loosely at the throat. He smiled at her.

'I gather congratulations are in order,' he said,

wondering where he had heard the name Cunningham before. But she was looking past him, astonishment plain on her face.

'Good Lord. Is that Graham, Graham Thoroughgood?'

'Yes, it is. He's the Clyst skipper.' He recalled their conversation before the match. 'He did mention you. He . . .'

But she was out of the car walking gracefully and without haste across the grass. Thoroughgood met her, hands outstretched.

'Dolly Cunningham. What on earth are you doing here? I haven't seen you for years.' Thoroughgood turned to Gauvinier.

'If this isn't the most amazing series of coincidences. Just one damn gin after another.'

'What do you mean, Graham? Mr Mitterman and I have just signed a most interesting contract. I came up to watch the end of the match.'

'But you never liked cricket, Dolly.'

'I used to.' She hesitated. 'When Mr Mitterman told me, it reminded me . . .'

'Just you wait there,' Thoroughgood interrupted quite roughly. 'There's someone I want you to meet.' He turned and ran into the pavilion.

'What an extraordinary man,' said Mrs Cunningham. 'I don't meet him for ten years and he suddenly rushes off saying, "You've got to meet somebody." What can he mean?'

Gauvinier stayed silent. He wondered what would happen.

Thoroughgood emerged from the pavilion, holding by the arm Fanshawe, still upright although leaning heavily now on his stick. It had been a long afternoon, umpiring out there in the sun. He had obviously not been told whom he was to meet. He looked inquiringly at the glamorous stranger, and stood politely, waiting to be introduced. Thoroughgood seemed to have lost his voice. Gauvinier put a hand on Fanshawe's arm.

'Oliver,' he said. 'I think you two know each other.'

He saw her eyes were violet blue. Gauvinier, Thoroughgood, Mitterman and the cricket field had ceased to exist for either of them. Fanshawe thrust his stick behind him and stood to his full six feet.

'Dorothy . . . Dolly . . . Dorothy,' he said.

Dorothy Cunningham held out both her hands. Fanshawe, suddenly looking his age again, held them with one hand, leaning heavily on his stick.

'It's been so long,' he said.

She came into the present, still holding his hand in her two. She looked at the cricketers.

'I'm sure these gentlemen won't mind,' she said. 'Oliver and I were engaged forty-two – no, forty-three years ago. But I haven't seen him since. We've a great deal of catching up to do.' They walked slowly to her car.

Thoroughgood could contain himself no longer. 'What a *bloody* amazing day,' he said forcefully. 'What a bloody amazing match.'

And Gauvinier, thinking it over later, could never quite make out what he was referring to.

They fêted Gauvinier in the Dun Horse that night, and he fêted them back. He was fined a jug for making his fifty and another for not making his hundred. Brewster, the big blacksmith, was fined a jug for his fifty, and took it as a yard of ale in the long flute-like glass that hung on the pub wall, pouring it down his throat in one long swallow; the first time any of them had ever seen it done. They had fined Budgeon for taking four wickets, not five; and for dropping the catch which put him off the field. They fined Larkin for his seven wickets, and Gillian for her second stout innings, and Deacon twice, for three wickets and for getting a duck. They fined Trine for his duck too, and Veysey for his unparsonlike exit. They fined Paul White for his run-out, and for his walkabout. And Jess for his duck too. And later on, long after closing time, they fined Fanshawe too, for not being fined before; but he was holding hands with the girl he had refused to marry forty-three years ago and didn't hear; so they fined him for not hearing; and Thoroughgood proposed a toast to 'the happy couple' which Fanshawe, waking up, excoriated as 'sentimental nonsense'. And then the little round landlord of the Dun Horse, who was growing worried for his licence (Clyst St Cob did not field the local policeman in their team) bustled them all out into the night. So the two teams, arm in arm, circled the cricket field in the full moonlight and sang 'Little Brown Jug' and 'My Old Man's a Dustman' at the tops of their voices until the local police sergeant did appear, wheeling his bicycle.

'Come along now, gentlemen and ladies. Come along. It's time you were all in bed. And you, sir,' looking at Thoroughgood, 'I'd have thought you'd have known better.'

'Don't worry about me, officer,' said Thoroughgood, peering at him. 'I'm, hic, quite all right.' And he sank slowly to the grass, gripping the sergeant round the knees. He was fast asleep by the time he hit the ground.

'Drunk,' said the sergeant reflectively. 'Drunk; like the rest of you.' He had watched the end of the match, leaning on his bicycle. 'Well, it's on a private cricket field and not on the public highway, and I don't think there's a law against that. So if you gentlemen' – he addressed the Clyst contingent, which was beginning to sober up slightly – 'would kindly go home without any more disturbance, we can leave Mr Thoroughgood to sleep it off. It's a fine night and don't look like rain. And you . . .' He addressed the Tillingfold revellers who showed very few signs of sobering up. 'If you, ladies and gentlemen, would care to get in your coach and spend the rest of the night there . . . quietly . . . then we'll just say no more about it. But I would advise you not to move either of these vehicles until the morning. I doubt there's one of you fit to drive. So if I see a movement on the highway, you can be sure you won't be going farther than the nick. I've never locked up a cricket team before,' he murmured as he ushered them into the coach. 'Good night, ladies and gentlemen.'

Some time before dawn had fully broken Dorothy Cunningham disengaged herself gently from her ex-fiancé's arms and sat up. The coach seats were not designed for sleeping in. She was stiff and aching.

'I must go,' she said. 'It would never do to let my board know I'd spent the night like a groupie in a cricket club's bus.'

'When will I see you again?' Fanshawe was only half awake.

She kissed him gently, smoothing the lined face.

'Someone's got to tidy up your dusty old Wisdens.'

She stepped out of the coach and carefully past the still slumbering body of Thoroughgood, then quietly drove her BMW away.

Half an hour later Gauvinier awoke with a blinding headache. He eased Gillian's head off his shoulder without waking her and stretched himself, looking at his watch. 5.30 a.m. They had intended to be home by now. He looked round at the sleeping, sprawling bodies.

'Not a pretty sight,' he said to himself. Even Gillian was hunched up ungraciously. At least, Gauvinier noticed, her mouth was closed in sleep. He wondered if indeed he was falling a little in love with her, and shook his head at the thought. It was a mistake. His head ached abominably and his mouth was dry. He stepped down from the coach. Not six yards away Wing Commander (Retired) Thoroughgood slept on, his head pillowed on his arms. Gauvinier touched him gently. He didn't feel cold. Gauvinier looked around him and went across to the pavilion. The door was unlocked. He found two umpire's coats hanging on a door and the remainder of an old sweater on a wooden locker. He took them and gently covered Thoroughgood as best he could. Then a thought struck him. Back in the pavilion he found three stumps, Brewster's broken bat, and an old ball. With some difficulty he set up the three stumps in the turf by Thoroughgood's head, placed the ball by them and leaned the bat against his stomach. His headache was gone, and he felt about fifteen years old.

Then he quietly woke Frank Hunter.

'Time to go home, Frank. Let's find somewhere for breakfast.

Hunter started up the coach, the deep thrumming of the engine slowly arousing the players from their various dreams. As it pulled away from the ground Gauvinier leaned from the door and gave the still sleeping figure of Thoroughgood a farewell salute. The stumps stood proudly at his head, the broken bat sagged at a wild angle across his stomach.

Each travelled with his own thoughts.

Hunter, behind the wheel of the coach, thought: Bit of a bloody waste of time, this touring. Not many runs, not many wickets. Give it a miss next year.

Trine thought: I wonder why Quim didn't turn up last night. Still, she'll come to the Chelsea Arts Ball. She promised that. I'll remember that catch for a long time. Pity I didn't make any runs. Wonder how I missed that dolly-dropper? That young ass, Paul. Pretty girls, though.

White thought: I showed them. That look on Jess's face when I gave him back his jacket. That'll teach him. That run-out . . . great.

Mitterman thought: How very satisfactory. Very well arranged, though I say it myself. Tour, deal, everything. Well done, James.

Deacon thought: Those stumpings were bloody good . . . We could have won that match if I'd batted properly . . . Wonder if Gina will remember me. It's only a week, after all. I could do with it, now.

Norman thought: Oh Bella, I'll see you in four hours. Bella.

Jess thought: It's better than touring with the group. Give me Wym or Clyst St Cob any day. But not Trewartha. It's all a bit earnest there. Those Cornishmen can sing, though.

Bason thought: I hope Frank's not going to go to

sleep behind the wheel.

The Reverend Richard Veysey said his prayers and tried not to think of the responsibilities awaiting him in Tillingfold.

Bobby Bewers thought that he must practise more in the nets. Get the slow bowlers to toss them up. Like that Larkin.

Gillian thought: I'm glad I came. It was all worth it. I wonder if I'm going to fall for Peter. He's the only one I could. But he's too nice. My first fifty. What a game. What two games, she thought ungrammatically. How do you bowl a cutter?

Fanshawe didn't think. He was still in a land of dreams he thought he had lost forever.

Budgeon thought: My bloody knee still hurts. But that wicket. I've never bowled as well as that before. Oh well, back to it. And the tax man.

Gauvinier thought: It was worth it after all. Long time since I've scored eighty. Should have made it a century. It would have been my third. Next time, we must give ourselves more time. A round of golf. A bit of swimming. Not so much cricket . . . Wonder if I'm falling for Gill? Polly will laugh at me. Bloody old fool. Don't feel fifty. I wonder how Thoroughgood feels now.

And so Hunter drove them back to Tillingfold.